Girl on Wheels

by

Tom Ireland

A Malinding Village story

Published for Gambian Occasional Emergency Support (GOES)
December 2016

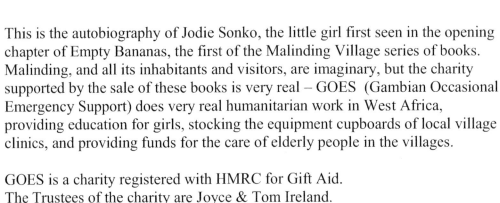

This is the autobiography of Jodie Sonko, the little girl first seen in the opening chapter of Empty Bananas, the first of the Malinding Village series of books. Malinding, and all its inhabitants and visitors, are imaginary, but the charity supported by the sale of these books is very real – GOES (Gambian Occasional Emergency Support) does very real humanitarian work in West Africa, providing education for girls, stocking the equipment cupboards of local village clinics, and providing funds for the care of elderly people in the villages.

GOES is a charity registered with HMRC for Gift Aid.
The Trustees of the charity are Joyce & Tom Ireland.

More information about the Charity, and about Gambia, can be found on the blog
GambiaGOES.blogspot.com

Chapters
1
2
3
4
5
6
7
8
9
10
11
12
13
14
15
16
17
18
19
20
21
22
23
24
25
26
27
28
29
30
31
32
33
34
35
36
37
38
39
40
41
42

And a total of 55,648 words

1

Hi, it's me, Jodie. Well, that's how I start my tweets (Rachel showed me how) so that's how I'll start the book. Almost thirty words already. Don't get it right, get it written, that's what Karen said and I always do what teacher tells me. Quite often, anyway. See, fifty words now. Let's get the jargon out of the way first, shall we? Then you can decide if it's worth your while to read on. OK? Right. I'm 28 years old, IC3, T10-L1, 1.45m tall, 62kg. heavy, a 2.1 degree, demographic class C2, favourite vehicle is my custom-built 6kg chair, and I play rugby to relax. Let's move on.

One hundred and nine words and you already know a fair bit about me. I reckon I can finish this book in under a thousand words. Fifteen hundred tops. That photo of me on the front cover? Yes, a bit out of date. I don't like any that's been taken of me since then. Twenty-one years ago I loved life. Didn't know that, of course, I just got on with it. School was good; I loved hearing stories and poems. I liked games and swimming - we all learned to swim. Then it all went wrong: mum died. She'd been too busy to go to the doctor about the pains in her chest. Then she dropped dead. Just collapsed and died. Gone. I was sitting at the kitchen table and she was fetching my dinner from the microwave. She sort of gasped, looked at me, tried to speak. I sat there, thought it was some kind of joke for a moment. I grabbed the phone and called 999. I tried to turn her over into the recovery position - we'd learned about that in school - tried the kiss of life and the paramedics had to drag me off her. I ran. That was all I could do. Just ran and ran and ran. The police found me - that was where I first heard the IC3 bit.

Three months in and three hundred and forty nine words. Where did all that come from? My memory is still mostly crap. My specialist - get me, 'my specialist' - says bits may be gone forever, bits may come back. It's a random thing, it seems. I'm advised to avoid any more accidents. I guess you could say that to anyone and they wouldn't take blind bit of notice. How do you avoid accidents? That's the nature of accidents, they happen without warning. If what's name, the Paedo, could have known that if he took that particular corner slowly he wouldn't have hit that patch of oil, which, because he was by nature a fool and hadn't bothered to replace three badly worn tyres, he wouldn't have skidded out of control and hit that crumbly old brick wall and he and his wife, my foster carers of the day, might still be alive and molesting another little girl and I wouldn't have been the proud possessor of a broken back - that's the T10 bit.

2

'Don't remember, I don't remember.' That's my fall back phrase. That and 'I don't know.' I know it sounds stupid. Being stupid is a great camouflage. People expect me to be stupid. Default position: default, not fall back. Give me time and I might get there. I don't remember, I don't know. It's the truth. I told you quite a lot about me and really, it's mostly things people have told me. I was seven years old when I knew I was different. 'Young female, IC3, recovered,' I didn't know that policewoman was talking about me. I'd only been called 'Jodie' or 'darling' or 'precious' or 'cookie face' before that. I liked the biscuits Mum made. Cookies, she called them. I ate them straight off the tray as she brought them out of the oven. Medium brown, sweet and spicy, When I was in my first care home I tried to remember her by going down into the kitchen one night. I just mixed all the things that tasted nice or smelled nice together and put the mixture into a bowl and put it into the oven. I turned the heat up as high as I could and waited for the magic to happen. It smelled quite nice at first, then suddenly the fire alarm went off and I was a stupid black bitch and what was I trying to do, kill all the good people who were going through hell because I was a stupid black bitch and I should be sent back where I came from.

'Please, yes' I shouted. 'Twenty-seven Rushgreen Street, please, my mummy will be there…' They wouldn't let me have my biscuits, either. One of the care assistants said she'd sit in my room until morning to make sure I didn't try to kill everyone and then take me to the Ed Psych because I was sub-normal. I don't remember anymore. Maybe I just went to sleep, perhaps. I don't remember.

3

Some people ask me almost as soon as we've met, others, people I've known for years, never mention it. I've never willingly talked about it. What am I on about? It's the crippled elephant in the room.

'What happened to you?' It's the question I try to dodge, but Rachel says I should face it and move on. I think I've moved on quite nicely without facing it, but here goes. Well, I'll try.

I left the writing at this point for a month. I lie. For two months. Sometimes I opened this file, looked at it, and then closed it again. Maybe I do need a therapist. I was offered enough of them when it happened, but I just couldn't talk to them. There was one guy, a youngish chap; I'd have been very keen to talk to if he hadn't been a therapist. I'd have been delighted to do more than talk to him. Maybe writing this will turn out to be therapeutic. Maybe that's why Rachel wants me to try. Devious girl, Rachel. Maybe. See, I'm rabbiting on instead of grasping the nettle. Nettle? Barbed wire. Razor wire. New paragraph and I'll try again.

I don't fucking remember. I don't have an actual memory of the event. Episode. Incident. Whatever: it's a blank. I just know that one moment I'm running down the garden and the next moment I'm waking up in hospital and it's the wrong day. People tell me I was in Paedo the Plank's car and he'd crashed it and he and my foster mum are dead. People tell me that but I don't know it. It's a story in a book but it's not my story. I don't remember being in that car, driving along that road, being terrified of heading for that brick wall, being trapped, being rescued, being like this. The last memory I have of Paedo the Plank was of him trying to get his fingers into my knickers again. He was always trying, any chance he could get, while she was out of the way. Maybe that was why I was running down the garden, it was an escape route. Over the fence, across the road and into the park by the canal. But I have no idea, no fucking idea, if that was even the same day as the crash. And there's nobody who can tell me. And now there's nobody who can tell me but I've got these wheels to remind me.

I told you how my real mum died. I've got the photo. It's me, of course. But I can see her, holding the camera, pulling a face to make me smile. I can see her better if I close my eyes. I don't have a real dad. I don't know if he's alive or dead. He's always been dead. I used to dream that he was a handsome African prince, a great chief, who'd had to rush back to his country to save the lives of all the children from a monster crocodile. I almost believed it. Of course he'd come home. He'd open the door and walk into the kitchen and say 'I smell cookies and I see my Princess' and I'd rush up to him and he'd sweep me off my feet. He'd do that. He'd swept my mum off her feet. He'd stayed long enough to plant me then he'd run away, she said.

Rachel told me not to bother, but when I was sixteen I searched for him on Facebook. I got his name off my birth certificate. I carried his name like mum had carried his child, tenderly, with love and hope. It's a common name, a sort of John Smith, but African. I found him. It took months, but I found him. I knew he wouldn't know me so I pretended to be mum. I waited a week for his reply.

He said he couldn't be responsible for every half-caste bastard on the planet and if I persisted in disturbing him he'd make sure my life would be short. Anyway, he only fathered boys, not scummy girls. So, I'm a bastard. I'm an orphan. An orphan bastard. A half-caste disabled scummy orphan bastard girl with a second-class degree and a chance to be in the Paralympics athletic team. Could be worse, Rachel says. She'd know.

How far did I get with my list? Facts and figures and lots of initials and numbers. That's how some people see me, statistics on paper. I've seen my case notes. Freedom of Information is wonderful. I didn't recognise me, but I think it boils down to 'she's a pain in the arse – don't bother'. There's one bit, prognosis it's called, they must have intended to redact it but it weaselled through. Seems I was going to conform to my peer group – prostitution, theft, drugs, and prison. Big mistake because I didn't have enough friends to make a peer group. They were right about the theft: I once nicked sweets from the corner shop. Old Mr Bojang caught me and gave me a long talking-to. He said that a young person of colour should set a good example to people. Then he gave me the sweets but when I tried to eat them they made me sick. I don't think shops are user-friendly to thieving wheelchair users. Prostitution might be a money-spinner. I get some very odd offers from strangers. Very strange strangers, some of them. Think I'll pass on that.

I wish I could remember more about my early years. One girl at Uni said she could remember being born. She was quite explicit. I'm glad I can't remember that far back. The photo I use on Twitter, though, I remember that day: Mum had been shopping – Oxfam or Save the Children – and brought these clothes home. I kept the hat for years; it was from some travel company. I got everything brand new, well, brand new to me. Flip-flops, shorts, knickers – still in the packet they were – two T-shirts and the hat. I wore the hat in bed. Mr Thingy from the flat downstairs came in and took some photos. There was one of Mum, but that got lost somehow when I changed from one foster home to another. I was too upset to cry. I keep closing my eyes to see her again but she's faded. I can still sort of see her, dead on the floor of the kitchen, but I want to recall her that day when she was smiling at me in my new clothes, telling me how beautiful I am. Beautiful, she said. Beautiful. Bugger, I'm not crying. I don't cry. Bugger. I've still got one picture of the happy day.

It was after that move, the one when I lost Mum's photo, that I went silent. Elective mute, they called it. I hadn't gone deaf. I'd been taken away from my first school, the one where I was happy, just after Mum died. Inconvenient, they said. If there was an inconvenient there must be a convenient and an out convenient too. Just a thought. So I went to a new school. It didn't look new to me. It was dirty and the paint peeled like an orange – you could peel great strips of it off the woodwork. You got shouted at and called stupid and Dumbo and monkey if you did that. They asked where your bananas were and could you climb trees and go jibber-jabber-jibber like a gorilla. And every time I opened my mouth to talk they shouted 'shut up, monkey, shut up', so I did.

 It's easy to give up talking. Maybe it made it easier, years later, to give up my legs. Rachel thinks that's a stupid thing to say. I could still run in those days. I could run and I could listen and I could learn. I knew I looked like a monkey and nobody loved me. Mum had loved me and told me I was beautiful but perhaps she was wrong. Silent was good. I got ignored after a while. They tried a Special Needs teacher but she was the one with needs. She needed to cure me, I think. The kids gave up taunting me after a while. I could run. Running was good. I'd run out of the school gate, along the road till I came to the footpath down to the canal and I'd sit on the bridge over the water. It was quiet there, and quiet was good. I fitted into quiet. I'd go back to school after a while. There was an iron staircase leading down to the basement where the boiler room was. Apart from the noise of the boiler it was good, lots of corners to hide round. I got caught there once. Three prefects, two girls and a boy, were sent to look for me and found me. They said they had a Science experiment to do; they had to find what percentage of me was black. The boy held me while the girls stripped me. It took ages to get his blood out from under my nails. When they left me I walked back to my classroom. I opened the door and walked to my seat on the front row. I always sat on the front row because the teachers said they wanted to keep an eye on me and help me if I found something was difficult. They lied. They really meant if I started to misbehave they could stop me. I explained the difference but I don't think they appreciated my help. It wasn't help, of course not. It was just me being a pain in the arse. Anyway, this day I walked in and sat down without a word. There was a gasp from the class, then silence. An alien sort of silence. Mr Rutherford turned and looked at me. For a moment he must have thought his eyes had broken.

'Jodie Sonko, Jodie. Where are your clothes?' He was taking his coat off and putting it over my shoulders. I sat still and let him do it.

'They're in the boiler room, sir.' You could see him struggling. How was he supposed to cope with a naked teenaged black girl starkers on the front row? I almost felt sad for him. I felt bloody cold too. A girl was sent to fetch a woman teacher. The woman teacher was sent to fetch a blanket and came back with a large towel from lost property. I stood up and returned the coat to Mr Rutherford, who shrank back from me. The coat dropped to the floor. The woman teacher wrapped the towel round me and led me out of the room. I stopped as she opened the door and turned back to the class and curtsied. It seemed a reasonable thing to do. The applause followed me along the corridor to the Head's office. The three prefects were waiting outside. I noticed the blood had dried on their faces. It looked nasty. I was put into a taxi and escorted back to the care home.

 I went back to school as usual the next day, no fuss, no police, and no expulsion. At least, not for me. We were three prefects short until three new ones were appointed. I didn't get an interview for the position but I suppose I was a bit too young. Maybe a bit too black as well?

6

I didn't sleep well last night. Correction: I didn't sleep last night. It happens sometimes. Not so often nowadays, but it happens. I used to have a carer, well, a series of them. They'd come in about nine o'clock and get me ready for bed. If they had time they'd make me a drink to take my pills with, have a bit of a chat, wheel me into the bedroom, heave me onto the bed and undress most of me. I hated it. I got rid of them as soon as I could. I manage for myself now. I used to hate going to bed. Nightmares, a choice of three.

Seeing my mum die. When it really happened I tried to help her, but in the dream I was paralysed, motionless, unable to scream. I was a pair of helpless eyes, unable to blink or cut out the sight.

Second screen was me sitting naked on the Paedo Planks knee, his hand up me, as we careered off the road into a solid cliff face, tunnelling into the cliff until we were entombed there, him bleeding all over me and me frozen into the solid rock, unable to move.

The third scenario was me at the controls of a plane, high in a blue sky, stunting, looping the loop, rolling over and over then suddenly plunging into a sports field where children were running races and playing rounders, all in slow motion, not looking up at me as I screamed and screamed at them to run away but they played on. Don't know what that was all about. Crash and burn.

So, at first, the sleepless nights were welcome. For a while. Then the thoughts came. About two in the morning, when I was begging for sleep, they came.
'This is how it's always going to be.'
'I'm useless. I'll always be useless. I'm a burden.'
'My mother died to escape me. I let her die. Why did I do that?'
'Nobody's going to love me. Boys didn't look at me before I was a cripple. No chance now.'
Now it's just me. I don't have friends. Wouldn't know what to do with one. Go shopping? Talk about boys? I don't do shopping, not with these wheels. I don't do boys either, and they don't do me. I've got a fair idea of what they might do but I'd need legs. All the girls in that book the Paedo Plank used to show me had legs. Legs and boobs. I'm a bit short in both departments. I do have bony elbows, are they any good? Two of them, one on each arm. See?

This writing business isn't as lonely as I thought it might be. True, I'm mostly on my own but the people I'm writing about seem real and they're in my thoughts most of the time. I was really most lonely when I was with people. Not my real mum, of course. She and I were really close. She seemed to know what I was thinking before I knew it myself. I miss her.

After she died I was very rarely on my own but I was totally alone. I was surrounded by people who didn't love me. School was worst. When I went into care they couldn't find a place for me anywhere near my old school. I went into a children's home miles away and to a new school. I was the only black girl there. Correction. I was the only black there. I was a freak show. That lasted a long time, and the girls were the worst. Girls can be horrible, two-faced, sly, treacherous, lying bitches. The teachers seemed to ignore me. I heard them talking about me - 'low achiever, special needs, anti-social,' that sort of thing. I looked the words up in a dictionary I'd stolen and I was not comforted.

I wasn't comforted when I finally blew up and attacked Linda Green. She was two years older than me and seemed to have developed a special hate of me. We were in different classes and different sets of course. I was in the slow achievers and she was in the alpha set. She was very pretty and knew it. Long blonde hair, blue eyes, athletic, class monitor - all the things I would never be. She seemed to dedicate all our out of class time to my destruction. Her nails scratched me, her fingers pulled my hair out, her hands stole my belongings, and her tongue accused me of all sorts of offences from theft to telling lies about her mother. She and her gang would lie in wait for me and hunt me down.

One Monday afternoon, as school ended, I snapped. She and her friends were waiting in line across the path. I put my head down, made a fist of my right hand, stuck my right arm out front of me like a battering ram (Roman ships had battering rams) and charged like hell straight at her. I heard them laughing out loud as I approached but I kept coming. I hit her full in the mouth. I knocked three of her beautiful pearly white teeth out. Blood was pouring down her face and from my hand. She stood, too shocked to move, staring at me. Her gang ran away, looking back at me, astonished.

She dropped to her knees, still silent. For some reason I tried to help her to stand up but she screamed. She went on screaming, scream after scream, till a couple of teachers turned up. I was weeping by now, repeating 'Linda, I'm sorry, I'm so sorry, didn't mean it, I'm sorry'. I wasn't sorry, I was terrified. Oddly, nothing happened to me, not in the way I expected. I never attended that school again. A couple of social workers collected me from the staff room and took me back to the care home. The following Monday I was presented to another school, one just for special needs children and a month after that I was in my first foster home.

I lasted a week in that first foster carer's house. They were a married couple, short-term carers they were called, I think. I thought their name was Foster. Mr and Mrs Foster, carers. They treated me like I was cut glass or something delicate. I'm not fragile, really I'm not, but I didn't know it then. They just seemed odd to me.

'Jodie, would you like ham or chicken?'

'Jodie, would you like to play a board game or watch a video?'

'Jodie, would you like to go to bed now or stay up a bit longer? Are you tired?'

How the hell should I know? Chicken or ham? What does it matter? What the hell's a board game? Tired? Yes, I'm tired of all this crap. You make your minds up; I don't give a flying fuck. At least I'd learned something at that crappy school; I was fluent in foul-mouth. I thought there was a town called Foulmouth. Everybody swore there and you got expelled if you didn't. And I knew what expelled meant.

Mr and Mrs Not-Foster lasted a week before they handed me back. I really want to get out of this swearing habit. Rachel says it makes me sound stupid and I should know enough words by now not to need the nasty ones. The nasty words help me let off steam now I can't just go for a run. I know I can go for a run in the wheelchair but it's such a faff, it's not spontaneous, it needs preparation -. I used just to be able to take off, really quick, less than a moment's notice, over the fence and away, faster than my thoughts could fly. I could run away from fear itself and find a quiet place. Just the joy of running and I can't do that ever again. Sod it, I'm young, I should be able to enjoy myself, feel my body working perfectly. It was the only perfect thing about me, that fact that my body worked like an express train. Joy was exactly the right word. I don't do joy anymore. Paedo Plank used to show me a book. Joy of Sex it was called. He used to read it over my shoulder and his hands would try to go to places on my body.

'Be honest, this feels good, yes? And this, if I do this?' But it didn't feel good. I hated it. I'm really glad that he's dead. I wish I could have seen his dead body, his corpse, and know that he was dead. They said I couldn't possibly be allowed to see it. If I'd been conscious after the crash would I have tried to save them? I tried to save my mum, once, ages ago, and I think that helped. The Paramedics said nobody could have tried harder, and even if that wasn't quite true – I was only a kid – it helped. I'd tried. But I don't know if I would have bothered to try with that couple. Maybe I would have just sat there, watched them bleed to death. Maybe I am a really evil person after all. I really think that I wouldn't have tried to help? That's not normal, is it? They were human, it was an accident, they didn't deserve to die. I expect they would have tried to save me, if they hadn't been dead. That makes them better people than I am. I don't think I would have lifted a finger to help them. Maybe I'm a cripple because I'm being punished. Maybe I can't run because that's the best way of punishing me? I asked a priest about it once. He'd come to pray at me just before one of the operations. So, I asked him. He laughed and said God didn't work like that and an angel had saved me so I could do wonderful things when I got better. But I'm not going to get better and run again. What use is a body that doesn't work? He just gripped my hand and smiled and the anaesthetic took over. Rachel just smiles too when I try to talk about it.

'Look at you' she says, 'look at you. Fastest girl in town on three wheels, just look at you!' I'm not going to swear because I wouldn't be able to stop. I'd rather I was the slowest girl on the planet on two legs. I might grin if I could wiggle just one toe. I might laugh out loud if I could wave one foot in the air. I might cause a riot if I could balance on two feet for thirty seven seconds, but it's not going to happen because I didn't do something to save two human lives. Life is not fair - or, perhaps, it is.

School got worse. I was the dumbest girl in a school for dumb people. I know it's not Politically Correct to talk like that, and maybe the PC police will come along and beat me up and throw me into a cell with angry rats, but that's how I feel. Before Mum died I loved school. I used to rush home and tell her what we'd been doing. I got a gold star for telling a story I'd made up in my head to the whole class and the teacher, Miss Ellesmere, asked me to tell the same story to the whole school at Assembly next morning and I did and that's what I got the Gold Star Award for. The head teacher even signed it for me. I liked poetry too, though I don't think I ever wrote any. I liked drawing and painting but I had a bit of trouble with some of the colours. Miss Ellesmere said not to worry; it made my pictures more interesting. My picture of green cows in a field of purple grass and flowers made some children laugh and I learned that pictures could be funny, just like some stories are. Miss Ellesmere said I was a very clever young girl with some special talents. I looked talents up in the big dictionary in the teacher's room. Teachers need a dictionary sometimes, so I felt really grown up. Talent could mean treasure, like gold, or being very good at something, or just money.

I loved Miss Ellesmere. I wanted to be like her when I grew up. I'm not. I'm ugly and foul-mouthed and stupid and crippled. Oh, and I'm black and that's wrong too. And that's why I go to a Special School that isn't special in any way you'd want it to be. Do you want to know what a Special School is like to the customers?

Well, the good things are that the classes are small, about ten or a dozen children. There's a teacher for every class and there are helpers, who help children who have difficulties, or at least try to. They helped Nicholas to stop trying to lift my blouse up and they tried to help Emma from being sick all over me and they tried to help me from being useless. They tried very hard and kept cheerful at the same time. I don't know how they did it: I'd cheerfully have murdered the lot of us. All they really do is make us remember all the time that we're not normal. What normal teenaged girl needs an adult to wipe her arse after she's crapped? They tried to use a special sign language because I still wasn't speaking and I tried to fail to understand what they were trying to say but somehow they cottoned onto that and we started to have some fun. There were a couple of other kids in wheelchairs, another girl and an older boy. We organised races and maybe that's where my competitive streak came from. The girl needed to be pushed but the boy and I were self-propelled and became quite serious. We let the girl win sometimes and she looked very pleased and laughed a lot when she came first. I accidentally spoke a couple of times when we started racing. I shouted 'No!' quite loudly when one of the helpers was going to push my chair. I wanted to win by my own efforts. The helper stepped back and smiled. She cheered really loudly when I came first in the race. My talking, if you can call one word talking, startled me. No harm had come of it; the sky hadn't turned to blood and the devil hadn't popped up out of the drain to drag me down play with Paedo Plank. I wasn't planning on saying anything else but it made me think. I accidentally said 'Thank you' to the teacher at the end of the day and he smiled too.

It's odd that just writing this seems to improve my memory. Sometimes it makes me feel really uncomfortable or sad and then, maybe, I'll remember something that makes me smile, something simple like saying hello or thank you. Maybe as I plod on with this book more memories will come. This worries me. I've built walls round me to keep things out, things like people, memories, dreams, ambitions. Walls keep me in too, isolate me, allow me to limit my horizons. They don't make me blind, though. I see. I see young women, about my age, walking hand in hand with their lovers. I suppose they're lovers. Why else would they hold hands? The last person I held hands with was Mum. I'll never have sex with anyone, so I'll never have a lover and so I'll never need to hold hands. How could I anyway? I need both hands to propel myself along in a straight line. If we held hands we'd go round in a circle forever and never get anywhere. But I was banging on about dreams a while ago. There's this new one. I won't tell you all about it yet, but it is a dream about a lover. I can't see his face but he's definitely a lover. My lover.

I was going to tell you about my helper. She's ancient, about forty. She's a teaching assistant, a sort of teacher but cheaper. They used to have real teachers like Miss Ellesmere, but the Special Academy sacked them all and took on a few cheaper ones at half the price. Academy; it's a sort of Greek word. A Mister Plato taught in one, ages ago. A grove's a clump of trees, like a small orchard perhaps. This Plato taught in a grove. The grove belonged to a chap called Academos, or something like that. So that school was an academy. A school without a building. Sounds a bit stupid. No, it sounds brilliant, so long as the sun shines. You wouldn't have to run away from school because you'd already be away. Anyway, this school I have to go to has a building and a security fence with cameras and doors which need pass codes. Mr Plato doesn't work here but the man who owns it, Sir Big Chops, has a sort of flat or office on the top floor. He never speaks to us but we see his wheels in the car park sometimes. It's big and black and it sounds an alarm if you accidentally nudge it with your wheelchair. Not that I would ever. Of course not. Only the once. He's a big man and he made lots of noise and used words I hadn't heard in school. My assistant told him off and he sacked her, there and then. She wouldn't go. She said she had a duty of care to me and if he said another word she'd call the police. I don't like the police but it did seem like a good idea. Sir Big looked at me and said sorry then drove away very quickly. He scraped his car on the fence so it was quite a good day really.

I remember another good day: we had a school trip to London. It must have been a nightmare for the teachers but we enjoyed it. Twelve of us went, three of us in wheelchairs and nine normal kids. It cost a fortune but my Trust Fund paid. One girl, Donna, said she let one of her uncles fuck her and then blackmailed him for the money. We stayed in a Youth Hostel right in the middle of London and we ran riot. Us with wheels were like greased lightning and escaped. By the time one of Hank's wheels fell off we were miles away from the hostel and a couple of nice police men took us back in their van. They put the blues and two's on and we had a laugh. One of our carers was really angry about that: we caused a lot of worry and the policemen might get into trouble for using the siren unofficially. Tough.

Something that wasn't exactly fun was a visit to a sort of museum for special children. I expected it to be boring boring boring like most museums are. They can't help it but that's the thing about museums. But this one was about kids like me. This museum was in a posh house with nice rooms and beautiful painted pictures and posh music playing, but it was good. There was a sailor, Captain Coram, who liked children. Not 'liked' in a nasty way like the Paedo Plank, but in a kind way. Turned out that long ago, when he was alive, there were loads of kids like me – not all cripples, but all orphans. Servant girls might be raped by their masters or seduced by men who ran away like my dad did. Lots of these mums just dumped their babies. Some became prostitutes to earn enough money to eat. Some were prostitutes to start with. Anyway, loads of unwanted babies. Most died. Lots of the survivors became chimney sweeps or servants or prostitutes. Captain Coram managed to get some rich people to fund an orphanage to save some of these kids. He couldn't save all of them so his helpers had to decide which ones to save. Some of the mothers hoped that one day they might get their children back so they left tokens to identify their child – a hazel nut or a bent coin or a scrap of cloth. It probably didn't help much because as soon as the mum departed, wailing tears probably, the child was given a new name and a bath and a meal. Because they got good food and care most survived. Lots of the boys went into the Army or the Navy and lots of the girls became servants. I expect lots of the boys died in wars and lots of the girls were raped and got pregnant but at least they'd know where to bring their babies to rather than flush them down the pan.

When I'd stopped crying about it Hank took me to the café downstairs – the museum had lifts so we could go everywhere. So, we went to the café. He bought me fruit juice and a big bun. The wall of the café had names printed on, names of orphans and foundlings. Romulus and Remus, Heathcliffe, Tarzan, Lyra Silvertongue, Frodo Baggins, and lots more. I felt at home. I didn't know then who all these people were and I thought they must be real, but they're not. Anyway, it was a good feeling. When we got back to the hostel Hank got me into a quiet corner and we had another good feeling. A grope. I was surprised how exciting it was. I thought the Plank had spoiled anything like that for me, and that the accident would have put most people off. But it had been a good day, not just the bit where Hank had his hands all over me but somehow the whole day was just right. I slept well that night. Strange, because I wanted to stay awake and think about everything. I don't even remember dreaming. When I woke up I felt like I was somehow almost normal.

Rachel's smiling at me. I've done something right. Or something write? This book seems to be a book about a book. How not to write a book? Do all writers agonise about what they're trying to say? Or do they just sit down in their studies, smile at the beautiful bunch of flowers their fan club sent, gaze out at their swimming pools, sip at a G & T and then write perfect prose at the rate of a thousand words an hour? What is a G & T? Must be something to drink if you sip at it. I've got this old laptop with windows 98 and a battery that lasts all of half an hour if I don't play games. Couple of hundred words a day? If I'm lucky. I once did five hundred but when I read it I was so ashamed. I shouldn't have thoughts like that. Rachel said I should have kept them in; they were what this book is really about. But what if one of my teachers - what if Miss Ellesmere - read it? Not that it's likely that anyone will ever read it, but what if? I wish I could keep this book in order, day-by-day, month-by-month. It keeps leaping about from year to year then back to another year. That last bit I wrote, about love and lovers. That was before I went to Uni.

I need a time line. BW and AW. Before wheels and after wheels.

Sorry, I came to a grinding halt after that last thought. Why do halts grind? Teeth grind. Mills grind. How do halts grind? Halt! Who goes there? An old lame lady, sir. She goes grindingly. I'm rabbiting on and on. Haltingly. It's a good job I've got Rachel to talk to. I'd be talking to myself otherwise. Going quietly mad. Stark raving starkers mad - like I did at school after those prefects assaulted me. I wonder what happened to them? I could make something up about them, I'm a liar: all writers are liars, well, the fictional ones are. I'm fictional, you know. I am. So's Rachel and everybody else I know. We're all a pack of liars. It's a bit like being a god, being a writer. What would I do to the prefects? You want to know? O.K. How's this: on their way home, after the head teacher had sacked them, they rescued a kitten that had fallen into the canal. They took turns to give it mouth-to-mouth resuscitation and wrapped it up in my skirt (which they'd stolen as a souvenir). They took it to the R.S.P.C.A. and it later found a good home with an old lady who lived a long, long way from any dangerous water. Sadly, on their way home after they'd redeemed themselves, they were trampled by a Mastodon which had escaped from a secret research centre and had to be shot before it trampled the whole population of Weaverham. It took years to breed another Mastodon from DNA and stem cells. I've just re-read that last bit and realised what a nasty piece of work I am. Still, I'm not going to change it. I hope it's not true …

Rachel's vanished. Maybe the last bit of the story was too far-fetched even for her? Maybe. She's pretty far-fetched herself; maybe that's why we get on so well together. If I had a real friend I'd like her to be like Rach. I know she's not gone far because she never does. She once stayed away for nearly a whole week. She thought I was becoming too dependent on her. But she did come back. She doesn't find fault with me so much nowadays. She used to be on my case all the time, day and night, but now we're best mates. She does give me that look at times and I stop and think what I've said or what I've done that wasn't quite right. Not appropriate kind of thing. I worry a bit about my state of mind. I was unconscious for a couple of days after the accident. I wonder if a few of my brain-cells opted out and didn't grow back. I never had that many to start with. I know I'm not normal. Normal people have legs and walk and run and dance and swim. I can swim, actually. Sort of doggy-paddle a lobster might do. My instructor thought it was a variety of butterfly-stroke, so that's it then: the halting-moth crawl. It works, gets me from one end of the pool to the other.

I drove past a hospital today, on the way to the travel agent. Yes, I do know I can plan it all on line, and sometimes I have done. But when it comes to handing over all that money I prefer to do it face to face. OK, I know, I know. I'm a Luddite. I just prefer people to technology. Except in hospitals. They should just have machines there. You could roll into a ward, through a scanner. By the time you arrived at a cubicle you'd be assessed, diagnosed and have a treatment plan in place. You'd be conducted to the appropriate treatment area and the robot surgeon would get to work. Simple. I hate hospitals. I've spent so much of my life in them.

After the accident I woke up in one. I wasn't frightened at first. I'd been asleep and now I was waking up. Bright lights - mum would be cross, it cost money to keep lights on all night. I couldn't see her; there were too many people there, all dressed as ghosts. I tried to call out, shout for Mum. I couldn't move. I must still be asleep, it must be a nightmare. Somebody was saying my name, over and over again. But I didn't recognise the voice, it wasn't mum and it wasn't Miss Ellesmere and it wasn't Rachel. The voices were talking about somebody called 'She'. Was Mum coming for me? It all faded out, the lights dimmed and the voices faded. I tried to stay awake but I couldn't. I was fading, disappearing, out of it. I was running across a field, jumping a fence, slipping a little, regaining my stride, up along the rutted stony path to the bridge. Nobody came here; I am the first human for a hundred years, maybe a thousand. This is my patch of sky, my plot of land, my old stonewall. The stretch of weeded water flows to my command; my people are ducks and butterflies and small brown fish. I am a discoverer, and explorer, the ruler of this empty land. There was one human here, just once, a long, long, time ago. So long ago it must be history now. We didn't speak, perhaps he sensed I was the Queen, he treated me with respect. He smiled, he held up a drink can, smiled again. I took the can and retreated to my wall. The sun smiled, the drink was sweet. I made a progress, as queens do, returned the empty can to the old man. He sat in the boat and slept. I quietly placed the can on the deck of the boat and silently ennobled him. 'Sir Man, Giver of Gifts'. He would be famous when the time was right. I forget the rest of the dream. Perhaps it wasn't a dream? It must have been, a dream of the past, when I could run and jump and play and dream. I don't remember waking up. Perhaps I haven't?

It bothers me, this loss of memories. I don't remember anything about the day of the car crash, but I have a car-crash dream. As far as I can check with the police and ambulance crews who rescued me, my dream is nothing like what really happened. I'm not sure I have a true memory even of being in hospital. Maybe my brain invented things to fill in the gaps. Now I'm pulling in to the parking place near the Travel Agent. Disabled parking. I should travel more by bus or taxi. There are special taxicabs that can take wheelchairs, and lots of busses have ramps. Honestly, I do use them, sometimes. But they won't let me drive the bus or the taxi and I hate depending on people. Rachel calls me bloody-minded. So, I struggle with this car, only it's not a car. It's my mobile world, my little inter-planetary shuttle, and I love it. It looks like a van, but it's not. It's my big wheels, automatic, with sensors all around to help me not demolish things. It's a space ship carrying my little wheels, and I launch myself across the road to the Travel agents who are waiting with the door open, ready to collect my tickets to freedom. I'm going to find my roots. Maybe not roots? A few twigs will do.

Strangely that car crash was the making of me. Not that it seemed like it at the time, nor for years afterwards. I've picked up my tickets from the travel agent. I've paid the excess excessive baggage charge for my wheels. I'm home now. The van's parked at the back, in my extra wide parking bay, annual charges apply. I can swivel my driving seat round, and scramble into my wheels. Then, providing I can find the remote control, I can open the tail gate, lower the ramp, and pootle back onto ground level. Hoist the ramp, close the tail gate, arm the alarm – and trust me, it alarms the whole of Warrington if anyone interferes with it! How do I know? Trust me, I know. Ask me who left her shopping inside and thought it would be possible to pop out and collect it? Without switching the alarm off? That's how I know. That's how I met most of my neighbours. At one o'clock. In the morning.

It seems that after the crash there was a lot of money coming my way. A very lot. Quite a lot of the very lot went on my care but there was enough left to buy the flat and the van and pay for my Uni fees. There was even some left over in a Trust Fund. It pays a sort of monthly pension but I can't touch the capital. I might just blow the lot and set up a brothel for strange gentlemen. Sorry, strange gentlemen. No chance. Writing this, this, what d'ye call it, this autobiography reminds me what an obnoxious little tart I was. No wonder I hadn't found any friends. I seem to have fought and sworn my way through school. I was waiting for the world to love me, like me, as if I had a right to love. Mum was marvellous but I wonder now if I was a pain to her. Single mum, demanding black kid … looking back I remember she didn't have many friends. None, in fact. Her mum and dad never appeared and by the time I'd had my accident they were quite invisible, dead and buried. I suppose I could do a bit of research, you don't need legs for that, but to be honest, I don't want to know. Mum seemed happy enough without them. Maybe they threw her away when she got pregnant and if that is the truth they'd have wanted nothing to do with me. I'm fiction, not fact. Just pretend I don't exist, it's better that way. Everybody near me seems to die, I'm cursed. I'm one of those Juju children; I kill people by breathing on them. Even my goldfish died. I won him at the fair, the one-time mum and me went. It was great, roaring loud music and lights as bright as the sun and people swarming everywhere. There was blackness just surrounding the fair ground and I won a goldfish on the tombola. I called him Eric and he lived in a big jam jar. I fed him on breadcrumbs but he died. He lived with me for a week and I loved him. I talked to him and watched him swim round and round for hours. Then, one morning when I woke up and looked at him in his jar by my bedside and he wasn't swimming properly. He was trying to but he was wobbling along on his side. I thought he might be hungry so I gave him more crumbs and a little taste of marmalade but it didn't help. He was dead when I got home from school and mum told me there was a special heaven good gold fishes could go to. We tipped him into the toilet and flushed it three times because he was a special little fish and we poured his water in too so he'd have something familiar when he got to heaven. My mum died the next year too.

13. Or 12a?

When you've had one accident, no fault of your own, you'd expect that to be the end of accidents. Well, that's what I thought. I was wrong. I'd faced the fact that I didn't have legs, well, not that worked. If I was sitting up I could rest plates on them. Or books. I started to read books because they were one step up from total boredom. That's a laugh, one step. Legs as trays? You could put a cushion there and prop a laptop in place. Jodie's book of 4 things to do with dead legs. Give me time and I'll think of the fourth use.

Anyway, accidents. There I was, fourteen years old, never going to walk again, never going to speak again, never anything again and they give me a set of wheels. I'm lifted up and plonked down and strapped in so I don't accidentally run over my own legs if they happen to fall overboard. I'm shown how to un-strap them like I'm a total fool and somebody with brains has to do things for me. Great.

Saturday was good. Most of the staff seemed happy to stay in their hovels at the weekend and skeletons provided care for those of us unlikely to snuff it for forty-eight hours. I skipped breakfast (if only) and headed gently for the coffee shop four floors down. I'd made sure my yellow banner was hanging over the back of my seat and made sure my back was exposed to as many of the CCTV cameras as possible. I managed the lift all the way down to the ground floor and wheeled slowly into the café. I was quite well known there and the staff had been programmed to be friendly. I knocked over my first Americano to help them remember me. I managed to drink the next and eat a choccy bar without making a mess. I paid for both coffees and the girl treated me to the chocolate.

I whipped into the toilet and accidentally left my yellow marker in the cubicle. Oh dear. I created a sort of headscarf out of toilet paper and emerged, I hoped, as a totally different person from poor sad Jodie. The toilet paper gathered a few sniggers from a team of Rugby players nosily escorting a fellow player liberally coated in blood but I was out of the door, heading for freedom. The air outside the gate smelled fresher, a bouquet of diesel fumes and aroma of fried fish. I headed into town. Pedestrians were the main problem - they still are, twenty years on. I could work the crossing lights. I was free. Unfortunately I hadn't planned what to do next. Maybe I should become a politician? There were shops, but I didn't know what to buy. I needed money and a sign pointed down an escalator to the shops and a bank. What could go wrong? You're right, it did. The chair and I didn't fully part company - remember the leg straps? We sort of cart wheeled tits over wheels down to the lower ground floor. I'd done no collateral damage so far as |I could see. There were no motionless bleeding bundles spread around my landing site. I listened to a fat man describing my parentage and intelligence surprisingly accurately. I just lay there, trying not to laugh. My anti-merriment campaign was quite successful because my left arm was giving me hell. It seemed to be tangled up in one of the wheels and not enjoying the situation. The paramedics were great. Maybe I'll be a paramedic when I grow up. If I grow up and a couple of miracles happen. Working legs would be good and a brain a little larger than a flea's. Fleas seem to manage pretty well just being fleas but I'd like to be a fully functioning human bean. 'Jumping Bean' mum used to call me. 'If you keep bouncing like that, Little Flea, you'll be up and over the moon and I'll have to be there to catch you!' But she wasn't there to catch me when I needed her. Sam and Harriet were there, neatly in uniforms, cheerful in spirit and trying not to laugh while they untangled me. I asked them to take my picture before they extracted me from the wreckage, and they did. They splinted my arm, asked if I wanted pain relief. I said no, because hurting was part of being alive and I needed to feel. When about forty per cent of you has gone on strike you need to relish the fact that the rest is normal, is working, is communicating with you. It turned out that one of my legs was broken. Harriet spotted that. I suggested she should cut it off because then I'd be lighter to carry but she wouldn't. I wasn't going to tell them where I was living but they took me to the A & E department anyway. I was handed over like a parcel, examined, taken to x-ray, plastered and told off by another big bloke everybody seemed to treat with reverence. Just a bloke, and with no sense of humour. I drooled a bit again and hung my tongue out and made gargling noises. He suggested a career on the stage for me. Bugger, sussed again. The wheelchair was written off. Pity, a new wheel and some glue might have got her back on the road. I felt quite attached to her. After all, she hadn't tried to kill me in revenge for wrecking her. Somebody told me later that she'd been rescued, repaired and exported to Africa. I hope she found a gentle user, not an idiot like me. I expected to be confined to bed while the bones knitted or welded or did whatever bones do. Strap me down and dope me and I'll be a model patient. But no. Look, Jodie, a new toy. Another wheelchair. Wow. Big deal. But it was. This chair was thousands of pounds worth of gadgetry, ordered for a girl who had died before she could play with it. I was, they decided, going to mend quite soon so I could have a loan of it for a few weeks. I only needed the use of one hand to operate this beauty. There was a little joystick - one of the nurses got the giggles while she was explaining it to me. I didn't get the joke for years. This joystick, she said would take me to wherever I wanted to go. It worked like this, she said. There was an on switch and then all I had to do was to wiggle the joystick in the direction I wanted to go. Like this she said and wiggled it. The chair leapt forward and pinned her to the bed. It's a mind reader, she said.

Because the chair cost so many zillions I wasn't allowed out without an escort but we did go back into town. I was escorted to the lift next to the escalator of doom and found my bank. I'd cunningly written my pin number on my plaster, the one on my arm, so I managed to get a statement of my wealth. I checked the balance several times, looking for the snag. This was my current account. It was huge. I could buy an ice cream. I could buy a small car. I could travel round the world at least as far as the battery would take me. I bought two ice creams, marmalade flavour for me and raspberry ripple for Joan, my escort. We sat in the sun and licked my display of wealth. I knew I'd heard words like 'compensation, and 'insurance' but I'd missed the link between those words and ice cream. I asked Joan about taking ice creams for all the hospital staff but she reminded me it was a very hot day and the ice creams would melt and run away. But it was, she said, a kind thought. That was a bit of a surprise to me. I hadn't been given to kind thoughts since mum died.

We trundled back to the hospital. I knew people were trying to find a new home for me but I wasn't interested. I'd had new homes before. People felt sorry for the little black girl, even before I was crippled. They'd make a few visits, take me out to tea or to play in the park and decide I was just the person to heal their marriage or replace their lost princess or whatever. I'd be sent to visit them, usually over a weekend, dolled up like a little princess and told to behave nicely. I was a miserable little sod. I would have tantrums. I would break things. I would feed chocolate to their poodle. I would paint their pet goldfish. Heads would be shaken, frowns would be frowned, and long words would be used that I would look up in a dictionary and, for some bloody stupid reason they would try again with another innocent would-be family. 'I'm your new mummy' some stupid bitch would say and I would scream 'Oh, so you're fucking dead too, are you?' as I hurled their bowl of flowers at the cat. I think I was trying to tell the world something, but I don't know what it was.

Oddly, I did get adopted. It wasn't for want of trying not to. After I'd been released from the clinic I was sent to live in a care home for the annoyingly disadvantaged. I felt like an animal in a zoo – you know, the runt of the litter that no one in their right mind would take home. I wasn't just the runt, I was vicious as well. I invented grunge. It's easy enough when you live in nappies.

I was advertised, talked about on local radio, paraded at open days, even had a video made of me. I don't think any customers saw it. Maybe my smile did it – or the farts.

But a couple of people did keep coming to see me. I made a point of not remembering their names. They didn't have any children of their own and didn't realise how lucky they were. They first saw me when I was in the exercise yard showing off, doing wheelies. Strictly not Health and Safety. That was the whole point. They waved at me and I greeted them with the traditional salutation. I saw them again, having a coffee in the reception area with the boss. They were smiling at me. Gross. I ignored them. I watched them drive off in a battered camper van with GB plates on. It had a big sliding door on the side. Then they did something really weird. I was quite shocked. I'd never had a letter. Never. Then this pair of do-gooders wrote one to me. It came in the post, addressed to me. My name on the front, Miss Jodie Sonko. Me. The head warder gave it to me at breakfast time, in front of everyone. Why did he do that? Me, head wild animal, getting a letter. Handwritten. Blue ink on a white envelope. Two sheets of thick white paper, each hand written, just on one side. Blue ink again. What a waste. They could have saved a whole sheet of that thick, smooth, whiter than white paper. Why not use ballpoint pen like normal people? Then I got to thinking. Normal people don't write letters. Normal people, if for some reason they had to write a letter, to complain about something, they'd type it on their computer like the clerk in the office does. I didn't read it. I tried to seal it up again, I licked the flap where somebody else had done, and it sealed up. Good glue. Odd gluey taste, not unpleasant. I carried it round with me for a week. It slept under my pillow. For as long as I didn't read it I could imagine what it might say. Sorry, Jodie, your legs are fine. Just stand up and walk out of that shithole. Or, sorry Jodie, I'm better now. They got a new cure for me. Come home to mummy, love. As long as I didn't read it, it might say those things. But I knew what it would say. It would say that they were sorry but because I was such a complete tosser they didn't want to risk me destroying their lovely home, their lovely marriage, their lovely holidays in their lovely camper van. The lovely camper van with the big sliding door that might open wide enough so a teenaged girl and her bloody wheelchair might just possibly get inside, with a bit of help, and go off exploring somewhere. But I knew it wouldn't say that. Of course it wouldn't.

But it did.

Dear Miss Sonko,
 We have enjoyed meeting you. We love your courage and sense of fun. We would very much like to get to know you better. And we've been talking to your carers about this. If you agree, perhaps we could have a day out somewhere and get to know one another better? Please have a think about this idea. I'm sure we could transport you and your wheels safely. We had a talk to the man at the garage where we bought Belinda (that's the camper's name) and he's installed a sort of safety harness to make it safe for you.

Where would you like to go for a first trip out? The seaside? A museum? A nice cake shop? Would you rather go shopping? We could come next week and talk about it?

Very Best Wishes,

Susan & William Bliss.

Shit. Bill and Sue, you silly simple minded shits. I'm almost willing to take you on and have fun. Buy me a toasted bun and let's have fun fun fun in the sun for the rest of our stupid lives. I don't make friends. I can't do love. I'm broken, can't you fucking see that? Take your stupid little bed on wheels somewhere quiet. Get drunk and shag as hard as you can and make your own baby doll and live life through her, or him. Have a boy, they don't break so easy. You should be in the museum; you're the last of the do-gooders. And you're white. Have you even looked at me? I'm black. Midnight black, without the stars. And that name, Belinda? What's that all about? There aren't even any humans called Belinda. Get the nice man at the garage to take that safety harness out and get your money back. Buy a dog, one of those sloppy Labrador things with big doleful eyes. Get a black one and if it's a bitch call it Jodie. Or Belinda.
Anyway, by the time I'd read their letter the one week deadline was past. A dead deadline.

They tried again. They just turned up one morning, half past ten. I saw Belinda roll into the yard. Big side door. I bet they hadn't removed the safety harness. They weren't carrying buckets and spades. Not the seaside then. The head warden met them and they gave him a tour of the van. My nose hurt, I'd pressed it so hard against the window. Bugger, they saw me and waved. I gurned back at them and slobbered a bit. Should have picked my nose too. I am getting soft in my old age. Sixteen next month. They're waving. No, they're not. They're beckoning me to go out to them. He's pulling the side door open. He shouldn't be doing that. I know the rules here. I don't like them but I know them. Rules are like walls. There may be a few gaps in them but they're walls. I don't know the rules about Bills and Sues and vans with big sliding doors. Big doors hiding safety harnesses.

I was such a cowardly little cat. I've got my own van now. It's got a name. I call it 'Van' or 'That bloody Van' when it won't do as I want it too. Like when it got bogged down in mud trying to follow Roman Roads in the Brecon Beacons. A girl with a tractor hauled me out, and then drove off into the mist before I could say thanks. Probably a ghost; I don't believe in angels. What do I believe in? How should I know? I believed in Mum. She was there, everlasting, just there. Safe. Loving. Smiling. Then, in a nightmare, she was gone. I can't forget it, I cling to every moment of our life together but bits fade away. Maybe that's what happens to old people, when their memories start to fade. I bet they get worried about it too. But old people are supposed to forget things; it's what makes them old. I'm not thirty yet and my memory has huge holes in it. There are things I know I've forgotten, like the name of the man who took my picture - the one where I'm eight years old, wearing a new hat. But there must be things I don't know I've forgotten because the whole memory has evaporated like frost on the grass as the sun warms it. Maybe the accident killed those memories, like I don't remember the accident itself. I forgot how to be nice to people. I forgot how to love people. I forgot how to be me.

Writing this whatever it is makes me forget sometimes that I'm writing about me. Jodie as a teenager is from another planet. That Jodie would have told the girl with the tractor to sod off. She'd have tried to extricate the bogged down van all by herself, even if it had killed her. I expect the girl with the tractor would have called the emergency services and waited till they arrived and offered any help she could. That Jodie would have cursed and struggled and resisted and been rescued against her will because she didn't know any other way. Giving in to help was weakness.

The big sliding door of Bill's van was her undoing. I'm writing, and that means I'm thinking, of that Jodie as if we weren't the same person. We are and we aren't. That Jodie had known and loved a mother, had walked and run and laughed and suffered unimaginable horrors. She'd been raped as a child, had lost the use of her legs, had lost her mother and her innocence. It's like she's an ancestor, same bloodline, same DNA, but I'm not her. I don't do god. I don't know if she did. I remember a priest praying at her while she/I was in hospital. Reading over what I've written already I see that I've referred to myself as a fictional character, and that feels appropriate. That lovely, scary, sliding van door was the gateway. I was free to turn round, wheel back into the care home. I almost did, then I looked again. Sue pressed a button and a ramp, shiny aluminium, slid out from under the van. It sloped down, inviting, tempting. The three adults stood talking, not looking at me. I was almost sixteen. I didn't stand a chance. I wheeled a little closer. I might just have been headed for the gate, but I wasn't. I might have been on my way out to the shops, but I wasn't. I was a mouse, headed for the trap and that fucking ramp was the cheese. I heard a voice, Satan spoke to me.

'See that wire? There's a clip at the end. Clip it onto that metal hoop on your chair, just above your feet, see? Then if you press the red button on this remote control … yes that's right, it should winch you up the ramp … yes! Well done. If you want to come out press the big blue button with the down arrow on … no? Not yet?'

I was a goner. Look, there was a tap, over a steel sink. Look, a cooker with three gas rings and a grill. That thing with a white door must be a fridge. Windows with blue curtains. A wide seat, a sofa, also blue. The cunning bastards must have found out that blue was my favourite colour.

'Would you like a trip round the car park? A woman's voice. 'I can drive really slowly?' That must be Sue. She sounded posh, not like Bill. He had a deep voice, local accent, a bit rough. Sue's bit of rough. I knew the words but I had no idea what they meant. A girl's voice:

'Please, Sue, could we go for just a little drive? Into town, perhaps?' My voice, being polite. No wonder I didn't recognise it. I looked back, out of the doorway, and saw three grown-ups smiling at me. Smiling and nodding.

'All right if I fasten these clips to hold your chair secure? And there's this safety belt to slip round you, you fasten it into here, just down by your side. When you're in you slide the door closed.' Do this, do that. There's a catch. Whenever I travelled in the care home's mini-bus the head warder fastened all the clips and belts and things to make sure it was done properly for Health and Safety, whoever they were. I'm being treated like a grown up. There's a catch. There wasn't. There wasn't a catch but I was caught.

Sue drove. Carefully, but not slowly. She said afterwards that she was scared stiff. Scared that something might go wrong, might remind me of my accident, might make me decide I never wanted to see either of them ever again, might, might, might.

No chance; I was hooked. We drove into town and parked in a disability bay. I wondered who was disabled, just for a moment. Just for a moment I was a teenaged girl going into town with some friends. Normal, like normal people.

'Jodie, slide the door open, please. It needs a strong pull. Right. Right back till it clicks. Now, before you undo the wheel clamps fasten the wire rope onto your chair. Now, if you can reach down, there's a clamp on each of your wheels. Can you undo them?'

'I can undo three of them, Bill, but if you can reach this one it would help.' It would help? Who was saying that? Me? Couldn't be. Me, asking for help? Politely? Bloody hell, I've been born again! Never trust a big sliding door.

I rolled backwards out of the van onto dry land. I unclipped the rope and pressed the red button to reel it back into the van. I managed to half close the door and said 'Thanks!' to Sue as she closed it properly. We discussed where we were going. I wanted to go to the bank and draw some cash. Then we decided to go for a drink. Not that sort of drink. It was nearly midday so we went for a snack. I was going to pay for it. I didn't know how to say 'thank you' again but I could pay for a snack and they might understand that was my way. They did. We went into a café near the market. It sold all sorts of soups and cakes and you got a free piece of fruit with your meal so as to be healthy. I had thick vegetable soup and Sue and Bill had pea and ham. We all had a slice of Battenberg after we'd finished our bananas and I was introduced to Espresso coffee. It's made out of coffee beans, not coffee powder. It was a day for learning things. I was allowed to pay on condition that Bill would pay next time and Sue would pay after that. I agreed and then realised that meant at least two more outings. I trundled up to the counter and paid. I hadn't noticed before but the waitress who had served us, taken our order, carried the meals to our table, had only one hand. Two arms but only one had a hand.

She took the money, gave me the change and I gave her a tip and said thanks. I read her name badge. Alison, it said.

'Thanks, Alison.' She smiled.

I rolled back to the table and collected my friends. I was thinking about that hand. I was thinking about the arm which didn't have a hand. The girl used it to help balance things and she managed perfectly. I looked down at my legs. I steered into a litter bin. Nobody commented.

'Sue, could we please drive past your house? That's if it's not too far away? Doesn't matter if you've got somewhere to go …'

'No Problem. Just drive past?'

'Please.' So that's what we did. I asked if Sue would stop, just for a moment, so I could look at it. It wasn't a house, it didn't have an upstairs. It's a bungalow. That's an Indian word. I looked it up.

I lay awake for a long time that night. I was getting to know the new me. Rachel was there, keeping quiet. If I went on being the new me would I loose Rach? And why was I thinking about a god? I'd decided ages ago, after I lost mum, that there wasn't a god. The priest who prayed at me, or on me, in the hospital, hadn't made me think about god. But I had read a lot about different gods and all sorts of religions. Several religions supposed they were worshipping the same god but were busy killing one another to get his best attention. Most gods were blokes. When I was little I went to a church school but there didn't seem to be much in the way of religion. Every morning we had a little service. Miss Ellesmere played the piano and we all sang then we got on with the important stuff like reading and playing games and painting. But now I was thinking. In a funny sort of way I'd supposed that the god had died when mum died. They'd been the same thing. Mum the creator. Mum my creator.

Anyway, I'd shown that I could behave in a civilised way. I'd been polite, I'd had fun. I'd been treated as an equal; a young, inexperienced equal but an equal. Sue had shown that a female could cope with mechanical things. Maybe I should have known this already? That's what I mean; there are things I don't know that I don't know.

That young waitress in the café today. She wasn't disabled. She had a disability, like I have, but she wasn't disabled by it. She did her job well, both the personality bit and the physical bit. And she was wearing an engagement ring.

Until we were driving back to the care home I hadn't heard about LUCA. Bill had the radio on in the van but it wasn't playing music. It was a science talk programme. I'd never heard one before. I thought all radio was just pop music. This wasn't. Two guys were talking about the last unknown common ancestor. It was a single cell thing that probably developed into everything else. Like the bible says if we trace all out relations back far enough we would get back to Adam and Eve. LUCA is if we trace back billions of years we get back to this single cell ancestor. There's so much I don't know. I do know I'm thick because lots of people tell me. Do I have to believe them? That's another scary thought: maybe I'm not stupid. I do some stupid things but, but, but what if I'm not really stupid? What, and this is scary, what if I'm actually quite bright? It that better or worse? How would I know? Would it matter? And thinking about what if: what if it all comes good with Sue and Bill? What then?

I couldn't go on blaming a door, not even a sliding one, for changing my way of life. It's just a sheet of painted metal, with a strong frame and lined with nice blue carpet. It feels like carpet anyhow. No, not a door. The door led to somewhere good, but the change was down to Sue and Bill. And me. I changed. I must have wanted to or I'd still be in the care home till they had to throw me out. Like on that first visit to their house that wasn't a house. Bungalow.

They called for me the next day, early. Tricia, one of the carers, came along with us, just in case we needed any help, she said. I think she was there to sort of spy on us, see that Sue wasn't going to sell me into slavery or that Bill wasn't going to cut out my kidneys to sell to a billionaire banker who wanted a spare set, just in case. See, I'm gibbering. It's the monkey in me. And the fact I was so nervous I was worried I'd wet myself. Actually, that was the least of my worries. These pads are little miracle workers. Be honest, Jodie. I was scared.

So, there we were, four of us, chatting about things, not listening to the music in the van, pretending it was just another day, visiting friends. Friends? I didn't have friends. I just had people who knew me a bit, who worked shifts and got paid buttons to care for me. You don't pay friends. I'd have bought a selected dozen, I had the money. No, friends are … I don't know what friends are. I knew what mum was. Mum was love, unconditional. Nobody else could be mum. I looked at Sue, sitting beside me on the sofa. Maybe we were linked by one of LUCA's single cells. But if that was possible I'd be linked to Paedo Plank or to the African guy who wasn't a prince but was my blood relation. He'd done my mum and scarpered and I didn't want a link to him either. I tried to think that it wasn't me sitting, propped up with lovely cushions, on the sofa in this big bright room. I could see the garden, stretching away to a hedge, with what seemed like a field between the window and the hedge. It was bigger than the care home's garden, which was mainly a car park. School had a big field too. Mum's flat hadn't had a garden, just a parking space for the car she couldn't afford. Bill went off to make some coffee and try to find some cake. Sue and Tricia were chatting about something or other and I was left to be me, quietly on the sofa. Bugger that. I'd seen which way Bill had gone so I rolled onto the floor and started after him. I half expected Tricia to dash after me but she didn't, she just went on chatting. Sue winked at me.

I can't swim crawl but I can sort of crawl: it's more of a drag. I headed for the kitchen and travel was easier once I got off the carpet. I crossed the hall and the kitchen was just in front of me. Bill was loading a tray with a big coffee pot and a plate of chocolate cake. I was so well behaved. I heaved myself up to table-top level and offered to test the cake for him. The least I could do, just being polite. He cut a slice in half and fed it to me. I nearly choked but I managed. When I got my breath back I tried to say 'thank you' nicely but it came out in crumbs. I tried to collect the crumbs together with one hand but I lost my grip on the table and slid onto the quarry tiles. A lovely shade of grey, the tiles. It would be good if I could blend in with them and be a floor for the rest of my life. I'd be a very nice floor; I'd only eat cake if it was dropped into …

There was a strange noise. Bill was trying to stop laughing. I could have killed him. We floors can get quite aggressive, everybody knows that.

'May I help you, Madam?' Madam? I liked the sound of that. I'm a proper little madam …

'Yes please, my good man. Kindly return me to the gentry in the lounge.' Oh, god. I've gone mad. Bill bows, scoops me up like escaping jelly and carries me back across the hall and gently lowers me into place on the sofa.

'Morning coffee will be served immediately, ladies.' I'm too busy thinking to reply. A man, a nice man who isn't a nurse or a doctor or a carer, has picked me up, been kind to me, not mentioned my disabilities, not groped me, and carried me like he actually wants me to be ok and feel at home.

I guess we ate cake and drank coffee. I don't remember – I told you my memory was rubbish. I was trying to get over the fact that two normal, probably normal, no, couldn't be normal, human beings, wanted me in their beautiful not-house with its lovely floors and garden and in their camper van with a sliding metal door. Why would they? Even now, at twice the age I was then, I can't answer that question. I still ask it, silently to myself, whenever they come to visit me. Especially when they come to visit me in Africa.

Africa? Ah. Right. Well, we'll come to that later. Let's get this bit of the tale told. I didn't get emotional till I was back in bed at the care home. I put myself to bed and burst into tears. What was that all about? Nice day out, full of sliding doors and cake and people who liked me, laughed at my jokes, asked my opinion, acted as if I was normal for a whole day. People who invited me back. That's not normal. I stayed for lunch, had a tour round the garden, and met the fish and the rabbit. Rabbit offered unconditional friendship but the fish ignored me. Tricia was keeping an eye on me. I sensed it whenever my back was turned. There must have been a little red laser spot between my shoulder blades wherever I went. I'd got that sussed: the care home wanted to get rid of me, and so long as Sue and Bill didn't appear to be child-molesting cannibals and were mad enough to take me on I'd be given into their care at the drop of a knicker. Was I crying because I might be leaving 'home'? This place had looked after me, fed me, made sure I was decently dressed, doled out pocket money honestly, included me in trips out and forced me to go to school, all for my own good. They got paid for doing it, of course they did. But they did it, even smiled some times. I hadn't encouraged that. There were rules. It became a game; they tried to enforce the rules and I tried to break them. Ever tried to get a wheelchair through a window in the small hours? Honestly, I just wanted to go for a run. Honestly.

Maybe that's what all the tears were about. Each tear a memory of a little act of care, even though I'd rejected it at the time. I knew this place and this place knew me. Is there a word for a sort of peace between enemies? A peace that was fragile, could be broken any moment, but could begin again a moment later? I'd been here for almost ever. I knew the boss warder and Tricia wouldn't harm me, not really. Paedo Plank was in the past, Mum was in the past, the kids who'd assaulted me were history and the girl I'd attacked wasn't quite a faded memory. Was I fit to live a life outside an institution? That young woman in the café probably managed. She wore an engagement ring so there must be a boyfriend? A fiancé, a hope of marriage, of children, of living a mutually agreeable life? She had a disability but she wasn't defined by it. Could I be like that?

So what was the matter with me? A nearly sixteen year old cry baby. For God's sake, a couple of visits, a snack in a café, a home visit and a few trips through doorways, sliding or not, to see what lay on the other side? Was that enough to behave like a, like a, come on, admit it, to behave like a scared little girl? Too bloody right it was.

Then disaster struck. I got a cold. No big deal? My life was destroyed. I don't get colds. Wimps get colds. Boys get colds. Planks get colds. I don't. I'm amazingly fit and healthy. I've never been ill in my life. Bits of me break or fail but I do not get ill. I just don't. I've had an accident or three but I have never been ill. I've heard about colds. You have a runny nose and sneeze a bit. You're all snotty for a couple of days and then you're well again. I've seen it happen. What day is it today? Check 'phone. Right, it's Wednesday. On Friday I'm going to stay with Sue and Bill for the weekend. A trial run. I've been packed for a week. Just the one bag. No, I lie. Just the one huge suitcase. Tricia lent it to me. If she stands behind it all you see of her is her hair. Still, just the one case. I woke up this morning and sneezed; it startled me. Then I noticed the headache. Then I noticed my nose was running like a tap. A bath tap. I was dizzy; the room floated gently round me. I felt sick.

'Got a bit of a cold?' Thanks, Tricia. I'm dying. My world is ending. I've never had a shag, I never will. I am death. I've never been to the seaside. I am seriously ill. I sneezed again and my head fell off. No, of course it didn't. Tricia went off to find a couple of aspirin. That's what they give people dying of a heart attack. I read that in First Aid. I am dying. Rachel has fled my corpse. She'll have a new friend by now. I hope they'll be happy together for a long time. I could plait these strings of snot into a nosetail. I will my body to science. Bill and Sue won't want me now. I don't want me now. The surprise they've planned can go to some deserving child. Oh, God, I feel rotten. And there's only half of me experiencing this disease-ridden hell. My legs aren't aware of it. As far as they're concerned they're still tucked up in bed waiting for nourishment. They'll never be nourished again. They'll just lie there, poor things, waiting, waiting, until they're bundled into my coffin and incinerated then tipped onto the rubbish dump for seagulls to feast on. I'm toast.

I was supposed to have a wonderful weekend with added surprises and plans for my future. Well, it won't happen. I've texted Sue to tell them of my expected early demise and thanks for all the kind thoughts. I've warned her that I'm highly infectious and snotty. It was a dream and you know about my dreams. Being part of a loving family with a room of my own and an anticipated holiday in a camper van with a big sliding door? Who am I fooling? Maybe a handwritten Christmas card addressed to the girl on wheels, if I last that long. My joints ache. A dizzy numbness pains my senses. I'll drink hemlock. It worked for what's his name. Bet it's on prescription only … Go away, Tricia.

'You've got visitors, Jodie.'

'No I haven't. Nobody knows me. If I've got visitors then it must be the undertaker so I must be dead. They've got my measurements in the office. Use those.'

'It's Sue. She's brought the hearse. Come on, get up. She'll drive you to the grave yard. Get a move on. Take this box of paper hankies … and plaster a smile on your face. You are not a pretty sight. Move, girl!' You can never trust care workers. They always have an agenda; life is good so get on with it.

'Hi, Jodie. We've moved the weekend forward a bit. Your room's ready anyway so let's give Tricia and her friends a break. We need to see you at your worst so today's the day.'

I liked her reasoning. I was too ill to be properly bloody minded. I gave in and grumbled sullenly. Sue was smiling at me. It's a plot. They don't really want me. If I go with them while I'm like this I'll say something or do something stupid and they'll bring me back here and there'll be a long sad meeting in the office and they'll announce that they really can't face the stress of having a potty-mouthed snotty black cripple soiling their toilets and dropping things all over the living room and shocking their family and friends so they'd like a pretty little blonde girl, a house trained one who'll smile and help with the chores and knows how to go to church and … and I break down into a blob of snotty tears.

I dressed. I rolled out of my cell. I rolled into the car park. Bill grinned at me
'Jodie rises, phoenix like, from the ashes!' I hate cheerful people. I ignored him. I let him
manoeuvre me onto the ramp and up into the van. The chair was clamped into place and I
was belted and buckled. He looked at me, serious expression.
'You're really under the weather, aren't you, love? You'd normally bite my head off if I tried
to help you.' Snotty tear time again. He let me get on with it. Sue joined him. I slammed the
sodding sliding door shut.
'Let's get on with it' I moaned.
They had been busy with the bungalow since my last visit. A glasshouse, a conservatory, they
called it, had been added to my bedroom. They were connected with sliding doors (more of
the bloody things) and another set led into the garden. The en-suite had been converted into a
wet room. So I could crap anywhere, I supposed.
'It's all right, I suppose. If you don't decide on me you can house anyone, cripple or not. It's a
bit classy for me. How long have I got to stay?'
'Jodie, it is for you. We wanted it to be a surprise so we couldn't ask you about colours, but
that's easily changed. If you decide to live with us, be part of our family, well, it's your room
so you decide.'
'Snot green with purple and puke yellow?'
'I'm not sure they have those exact shades at John Lewis, but yes.' What was wrong with
these people? I was a child. Children don't get what they want. They don't even get to choose
what to spread on their bread. I gave up. I wasn't well enough to wage a words war. The
sliding doors worked and I wandered out into the garden. A path led from my glasshouse
door all the way round the bungalow. Other paths branched off to the gate, to the garage, and
to a sort of shed at the end of the garden, but I felt too weak to explore. I rolled back into my
room and clambered onto the bed. They didn't rush to help but stood back and watched. I
pointedly slammed my eyelids shut and heard Sue and Bill quietly leave the room.
I lay on the bed and thought. Yes, I was a little bit poorly but they had sussed I was not on
death's wagon. They had done a tremendous amount of work on my room and I'd been as
grateful as a fart. And I was thinking of it as my room. My room. Not a room, my room. The
room I wanted to be in. The room in the house I wanted to live in. The room in the house
occupied by the people I wanted to grow into my family. It's amazing how a snotty nose can
make you change your world. I pulled myself into a sitting position and looked out at the
garden. I could garden. I could pull things up and put them in a bin. They'd like that. I could
get involved. Think the thought, act the action. Where had I heard that before? I rolled myself
to the edge of the bed and sort of dropped into the chair. The chair rolled away. Some idiot,
me, had forgotten to put the brakes on. I crawled after the chair and subdued it.
'You OK in there?'
'Fine, thanks, just going to roll round the garden.'
'Have you got time for a drink first?'
'No problem, in the kitchen?'
'Yes, come and join us.' Slide open door into hall, cross hall, slide open door into kitchen.
Bloody hell, they'd changed all the doors in the house. For me. They didn't want a pretty
blonde house-trained princess. They wanted me. I tried not to cry but gave up. Crying was
OK. It was safe to cry here. Bill pushed a box of tissues across the table towards me. I smiled
at him and couldn't stop crying.

Adopting me wasn't a piece of cake. Bill explained that to me. He didn't blame me, which was decent of him, but it was my fault. My fault because half of me was the wrong colour. Mr and Mrs Wills were, are, pure white. Me, I might as well be piebald or brindled. It would be easier if I was black below the waist and white above. I like my colour: sort of golden brown, with pinky palms and soles. My hair's a bit of a betrayal; I like curly bushy with a few dreadlocks. Blonde would be more acceptable. And I'm old; too many years on my calendar. I was interviewed repeatedly. I don't interview well. I tend to get a bit shouty, and I don't like to be talked down to.

'She certainly speaks her mind' was probably the least offensive comment I overheard. Nothing wrong with my ears, apart from their colour of course. My nose must be the wrong shape too; I find that patronising idiots with posh voices and suits get up it too easily. At least I was honest with them. Too honest. How can honesty be a problem to getting adopted? I did learn that there was coded language; for instance 'Any questions, Jodie?' really means 'That's every tick box ticked. Let's get off home!' Guess which prat launched into a detailed examination of their qualifications to decide my future. Come to think of it, I may have done exactly the right thing to ensure that Sue and Bill would be perfect parents for me. For one thing, they were the only candidates and for another, if this placement didn't work they might be faced with having to cope with me on innumerable similar attempts. I'd asked if they had to volunteer for this work and I also saw the looks they exchanged. 'That's a No then?' I said. Anyway, six months later I had a mum and dad, which was great. Bill and Sue had a daughter, which perhaps wasn't quite so perfect, but they seemed pleased. We went out to celebrate at a posh place and I managed the knives and forks quite well.

The suits kept a rather obvious eye on me. I don't know what they expected to go wrong, other than Bill might have murdered me, which would probably have been justified. I was mildly surprised that he didn't. If he had done me in he could have pleaded sanity. The insane bit was that he didn't. I'd sussed that we were both wind-up merchants. I'd also sussed that he quite enjoyed having his patience tried by a stroppy teen.

I love this couple. It took a long time to realise this, let alone tell them. But it was the best day's work I had ever done, that day when I dropped the words into conservation about something ordinary, like going to buy new shoes. I hadn't bargained on all three of us bursting into tears. Trust me to bugger up a shopping trip.

One thing leads to another. Sue asked me what I would like as an adoption present. It seemed a silly idea. Why should I get a present for getting something I had hardly dared to dream of?
I had clothes to wear, food to eat - and I could choose some of it - a beautiful room, two rooms really - and I was doing well at school. My tutor wasn't Miss Ellesmere but she was really quite good. Very good in fact. So I said I'd like a dictionary. A big dictionary. And there it was. Well, it wasn't an it. It was a they. Two big books, both part of the same dictionary. The SHORTER English dictionary, full of words. Bill was smiling at me. He smiled again at dinner time. Dinner time was at seven every evening. Teatime to normal people, dinnertime in the bungalow. They recorded The Archers so they could listen to it after we'd finished eating. Every evening. Mad.
I said he was smiling, didn't I? Then he said
'I've had an idea. Let's go and see a really big dictionary. What do you think?'
'Sounds a stupid fu…..' I managed to stop myself just in time. We don't swear at meal times. Not often. Only in extremis. I know what that means, believe me.
'We go away for two nights and eat cake. There's a ground floor room a bit like yours, a big garden, and a castle across the road. And a very big dictionary.'
'They really have cake?'
'Lots of it.'
'OK. If you really want to.' This is scary. I keep catching myself being nice to people. 'A sort of weekend away? A holiday? Then we come back home?'
'You've got it.'
'Right. When?'
'Tomorrow. They've got a room for you, like I said, and a room for us. I'll just call and confirm?
'We don't have to fly anywhere, do we?' I hated the idea of flying.
'No. Just an hour's drive. It is in another country though. They do speak another language but they all know English.'
'It's in Wales?'
'Not too far from Chester. Gladstone's Library in Hawarden. With cake.'
'Just cake?'
'Oh no. Lots of other food too. And books. And a very big dictionary.'
There are so many things I didn't know. I looked at my borrowed suitcase. It took up half the spare space in the van. How much stuff did I need for two nights in a cake library? There's a first time for everything.
'Sue, help, please. I need some help packing.' God, was that really me?
'Just a moment, love. I'll be right with you.' She probably needed a moment or ten to recover too. Between us we managed to pack everything, plus some, into a moderate sized rucksack. I like the rucksack idea, it feels expeditionary. Mum had wanted to take me on adventures, but she didn't have this sort of money so our expeditions were in fairy tales. No harm in that, and I wouldn't have missed our story times for worlds. They were worlds, in a way. I slept that night with the rucksack on the bed. I wasn't going to let the dream that might come true slip away. I was awake and taking a shower at five o'clock the next morning. My rucksack was waiting by the front door, ready for adventure, half an hour later. Me? Excited? Don't be silly. Breakfast, toast and marmalade, and coffee, all prepared by me, fully dressed, eaten and washed up, ready for the road by six. Where the hell were Sue and Bill? Snoring their stupid heads off as I waited in my chair in the hall. Half an hour later their en-suite loo flushed. Fifteen minutes later I heard their shower running and a lot of giggling. Insensitive sods.

Eight o'clock before they emerged, still in their dressing gowns, hand-in-hand heading for the kitchen. Bloody parents. Not fit to be in charge of a woolly wombat. Have they no feelings, no sense of occasion? Don't they realise the importance of the day? I bet they haven't even packed yet! I glowered at them. They didn't even bloody notice. And I'd cleared up the mess I'd made when I burned the toast.

'Morning Jodie. Come and talk to us?' Like fuck I will. I never want to speak to you two again. I can do silent for years. And more years. Just you try me… I joined them in the kitchen and they made porridge for me. I was ravenous. The coffee was good too. We chatted about how long the journey would take, that there was a bit of a problem: I'd only be able to easily access the downstairs part of the building because it was some sort of ancient monument and they couldn't yet fit a lift in, but Bill would carry me upstairs if I liked. I could come and go into the grounds and into the village, there was a bank and a village shop, and if I wanted to do some work, read or make notes or something, I could use the same desk all the time we stayed there. What the … would I want a desk for? It sounded more like school than a cake library. I didn't want to go. They could go. I would stay here. I could look after myself, couldn't I? I was grown up, wasn't I? Nearly sixteen, I could get married, couldn't I? Yes, yes ,yes, and yes! Still, going for a drive might be, might be something or other. No harm done. We arrived in time for morning coffee. The drive had been mostly motor way, with glimpses of canals and rivers and lumpy hills.

  The library was amazing. Think of a fairytale palace. The car park was full so we parked on the lawn at the front. There was a big statue of some dead guy - you have to be dead to get a statue, it's a sort of rule. I had the door open and the ramp down and out of Belinda before Bill had finished parking. I forgot the rucksack. I forgot manners; I just wanted to see inside this place. The door didn't slide, it was massive, solid wood. There was a small reception office just inside the door.

'Good morning. Jodie? Hello. I thought you were here with Sue and Bill Wills? I'm Ami, I'm on reception today.'

Ami was white, very pretty, and smiling at me. She stood up and shook my hand. I hated her. I hated all pretty white girls who could stand up and smile and make it look natural. I was about to spoil the moment but Bill and Sue arrived in time to save me. Ami was talking again. She even had a nice voice.

'Jodie, you're in room two, just past the dining room and on the right. Sue, you and Bill are in room nine again? Both rooms should be ready in a couple of hours. Perhaps you'd like to have a coffee or look at the papers in the Gladstone room?' They all looked at me.

'Coffee sounds good' I said. I was morphing into something strange. Bill led the way, up a short ramp, along a long corridor, turn left into the dining room. There was a long serving counter with cake on display. Chocolate? I scanned the stands anxiously. Yes!

'Coffee cake and Americano, black, please.' I was learning the language but it still sounded strange. In my other life coffee powder came out of large tins labelled "Economy Brand". Sue and I found a table. It wasn't rocket science; the place was a dining room. Groups of people sat at other tables, chatting, reading papers, one or two were busy with laptops or phones, a middle-aged black woman looked up from her paper and stared at me. She frowned, then smiled. Why would she frown? If they let her in, and she was blacker than me, why shouldn't I be there too? And what was the smile about? Was she laughing at me? Because I'm a half-caste, is that it? Or because I'm a clumsy cripple? Don't they have cripples where she comes from? I've every right to be here, probably more right than she has. I was born here. I spoke. Good morning.' What had become of me? I wheeled into the space Sue had made for me at a nearby table and Bill arrived with three coffees and three good slices of chocolate cake. I hoped there was some left for later. There was silence for a while. I pottered back to the counter for more coffees. Bill and Sue weren't one-cup people.

'I'll put it on your tab; do you have a room number yet?' I told her I was in room two and she did something at the till. I was waiting to reject her offer of help but it didn't arrive. I slid the tray of drinks on to my lap and wheeled back to our table. That black woman smiled again as I passed her table. What was her problem? We chatted. Bill obviously knew several of the people in the room. A few came to our table and shook hands. Bill introduced me as 'This is Jodie, our daughter' and the people smiled and shook my hand again.
I shook hands back and smiled and said 'Hello, how are you?' to each one. Most said 'hello and how are you?' back but I could sense that they didn't need a detailed medical explanation of my condition. It was just something they said. After a while Bill suggested that we go to reception and collect our keys and bags, freshen up and meet at the counter for lunch at twelve o'clock. I led the way. I liked leading the way. It was something that daughters should do for their aged parents. I knew how to be a daughter; I'd been one before.
'Hello again' said Ami. 'Remind me, which room are you in?' At least she didn't show off and stand up this time.
'Room Daughter' I said. 'Bugger, sorry, room two, please.' I heard Bill not sigh. He collected their key to room nine and Sue offered to help me settle into my room. I hoisted the rucksack onto my lap and had enough brain cells sparking to accept her offer. Mothers should help their daughters now and again, I reasoned. I was a little disappointed with the room. Perhaps I had expected something magical, fairy-castle like with a spinning wheel and cobwebs of spun gold and an elf. It was just a very practical, attractive, comfortable room for somebody who wasn't too light on their feet. The bathroom was enormous. But not magical. Not a broomstick in sight. Ah, well. Sue helped me strew the spare bed with the contents of my sack. No point in hanging things up. Bed level was good. I sent Sue off to organise Bill. Perhaps I should practise calling them mum and dad? I'd spring it on them some time, not just yet. Would they like the sound of it as much as I liked 'daughter'? Perhaps it had been a very cunning plot of Bill's to come away from home and try a few new words out, on neutral ground, like?   If they didn't work out quite right we could leave them behind and try again, perhaps, later?

After we'd had lunch, mustn't call it dinner, we sat around chatting in the big sitting room. Sue was catching up with some friends she'd made on a previous visit and I had the daughter treatment again. I noticed the black woman looking at me again, with a sort of cross between a smile and a frown. She was standing near one of the big fireplaces - doesn't everyone have two fireplaces in their sitting room? I was getting into the swing of big houses. I excused myself from mum's group; 'mum's group' - get me! - and rolled across to her. The frown faded and the smile widened.

'Sorry if I was staring. I'm Sirra Ceesay, from Malinding village, in the Gambia' and held out her hand.

'And I'm Jodie Sonko, from darkest Cheshire. My mum and dad are over there, talking to people. How do you do?' Get me again, all this white tribe ritual.

'Hello, Jodie. Is it OK to sit and talk for a while?'

'Yeah, so long as you don't try to …' I was going to say 'try to molest me' but I managed to switch out of potty-mouth mode. I could sense Rachel beaming at me. Where had she been for the past couple of weeks? Sirra smiled.

'No, nothing like that, whatever you thought'.

 I tried again.

'Do you live in a mud hut with a thatched roof? Are there lots of wild tribes fighting each other? Do you … ' I know when I'm being laughed at. As soon as we got home I was going to ask dad to sponsor me for a brain transplant.

'Sorry, Jodie, I wasn't laughing at you. Of course we don't do any of those things, any more than you do. We do have several tribes, I'm Mandinka. There are also Wolof, Jola, Serehula and Aku. Some people do live in mud brick houses but they may well have piped water and electricity. And to be honest, it's far too hot to fight. And to explain why I wanted to talk to you, well, you look like a Mandinka girl.' Was that an insult? Was it better or worse than looking like a girl from Widnes? I could hear Rachel telling me to shut up and listen. Fat chance.

'I'm here because my mum and dad wanted me to be here. I'm adopted. My real mum's dead. My legs are like this because I was in a car crash. I'm rubbish with books and I'm so stupid I'm a plank. I'm a half caste and a half wit.'

'Jodie, that's not you. I suppose you could call my children half caste. My first husband was a white man. He died a while ago and I came back here to help remember him. I've two children. My son is the Alkalo, the chief, of our village. He's also a university lecturer. My daughter is a lawyer and she's also a member of parliament. And you don't seem to be at all half-witted. You can listen, you can express yourself fluently and you're not afraid to ask questions. I'm a teacher. Don't look so scared, I won't bite. We have crocodiles to do that for us.' It took me a moment to see that she was joking. I hoped she was, about the crocodiles, anyway. I was having a conversation with a stranger. What was happening to me? I was having meals with the wrong names. I was being fairly polite. I was staying in the sort of place that normally wouldn't let me in. I was in the sort of place I didn't know existed.

'Sirra?'

'Yes, Jodie?'

'Tell me about Africa?'

'Don't look for the differences. Look for the similarities. Start small. Let's start with Malinding. A couple of hundred compounds - places where people live. Men, women and children. There are three schools, a clinic, half a dozen mosques.'

'Mosques?'

'Like your churches. We're mostly Moslem. One of the schools is the Koranic school, a religious school for children of all ages. One of the others is the nursery school where I used to teach before I became a lecturer. The last school is the lower basic, for children from the age of seven to twelve. Older children have to go to the next village, if they can afford to.'

'I hated school. I was told I was stupid and because I was black I got called names so I ran away. My ambition was to leave school. My mum and dad want me to go to college but I bet they won't have me.'

'That would be a great pity. Parents are the same all over the world. My father insisted I attend school. He worked very hard to raise the money. I went to school in the mornings and I worked in the garden with my mother in the afternoons.'

'Garden?'

'Yes, a place to grow vegetables, an allotment, I think that's what it's called here. All parents want the best education for their children. Because I had attended school and passed my exams I became a trainee teacher at the nursery school. I taught in the mornings and worked in the garden in the afternoon and studied by candle-light in the evenings. In between I helped to fetch the water and feed the chickens and do the washing and look after the younger children. I expect it's much the same here?' I gawped at her. I spent most of my days sulking and swearing. She glanced at her watch. Digital, plastic, five pounds from the market.

'Sorry, Jodie, I'm supposed to be working. See you after dinner, perhaps? Say 'Hi' to your mum and dad for me?' She shook hands and walked away, smiled back at me. I rolled back to my folk.

'You've made an impression there' said dad. 'Do you know who she is?'

'Yes: she's a retired teacher and she feeds chickens.'

'And she's a United Nations Peace Envoy and she's here to write a speech. She's also an ex-model and beauty queen and she has a PhD in comparative religions. And yes, she does feed the chickens when she's at home.' Sometimes my dad speaks pure gibberish.

'Right.' I said. I started fiddling with a chess set on a small table to the right of one of the two huge fireplaces. Somebody had placed the pieces wrongly so I put them in order.

'Do you want a game?' Some old guy trying to chat me up.

'Do I look as if I do?'

'Well, you are setting the board. I'll give you a game, if you like.' I came over all shy. And all rude. The poor chap was only trying to be friendly: he was far too old to be randy.

'Sorry, not just now. I was wondering how a game might go if each player could start with the pieces in any place in the first two rows? Say, some pawns on the back row and the rest mixed up. Perhaps you could place half your men where you like and half your opponents? Then play normal moves? If it was a real war you couldn't expect all your men to be in exactly the best place? Some might be on holiday or some might be in hospital? That sort of thing?'

'Wars starting with anarchy?' He was frowning; he didn't dismiss the idea and call me a stupid black cow.

'Well, keep the same move for each piece, just starting in a different place. Play tomorrow afternoon?'

'Right: your new rules, three o'clock?' We shook hands. He was wearing a dog collar and a purple shirt. He smiled and ambled away, pausing to shake hands and chat with mum and dad.

Dad looked at me, smiled.

'You do know who he is? No, of course you don't. He thinks you're an original thinker. You've made an impression, young Jodie.' I was always making impressions, like a bad dentist. Who could this old bloke be? I took a long look at my new mum and dad. It was the first time I'd seen them in a new setting. They looked comfortable, they blended in. I wouldn't have thought them out of place - that was my job. I could be out of place anywhere on the planet. Mum and dad just seemed natural, part of the scenery. The scene was a huge Victorian building, full of books and people who smiled and talked in posh voices. I hadn't heard anyone swear all the time I'd been here. People even talked to me as if I belonged, like that chap with the purple shirt. Now I'm being introduced to someone else, a woman, middle aged, grey, another writer, just had a film made out her book. Who are these people? Mum introduces me, her daughter, and this woman doesn't even raise an eyebrow: daughter? Me, black, on wheels, awkward as a cow on ice, talks in grunts, and famous writer just smiles and gives me a hug.

I'm writing this about myself but I could be writing about an alien, fictional girl. She's not me, I'm not her. It's like I was real for the first seven years of my life, while my real mum was looking after me, then I became fictional during my being fostered, having the accident, growing up in care homes and hospitals, missing bits of my memory, then getting another mum who came with a dad, a first for me, and they really liked me, thought I was great and funny and clever and, worst of all, believed that I was a real person. That's when I stopped being fictional. It's when Rachel disappeared too. I still miss her. I have to deal with real people, including myself, and it's not easy. When I left home to go to Uni a few years later dad gave me a copy of a speech from some fictional guy to his equally fictional son. I still remember the last bit of it: 'To thine own self be true, and it shall follow as the night the day thou cans't not then be false to any man.' I didn't understand it but it made me cry. Maybe I did understand it without realising it.

We had dinner and talked to more people and nobody swore at me or called me stupid or spazzy or kicked my wheels or even seemed to notice my faults. Odd: they all seemed quite bright. After dinner we three went into the library. It was supposed to be a silent place: I cocked that up - as soon as I got through the doors and looked round I went 'Bloody hell! It's like a monastery!' Somebody sniggered then coughed to cover it up. There were books everywhere. I signed in as a reader: Dad vouched for my good character, which made me wonder if he really knew anything about me. Sue wheeled me back out of the library and read the riot act. "An Act for preventing tumults and riotous assemblies, and for the more speedy and effectual punishing the rioters" How the fuck do I know that? I read things and remember them. It's a trick: I'm not clever or anything, I just remember things that don't matter and forget things that do. I forget the sound of my first mum's voice, or the sound of the car crash but remember bits of rubbish like the Riot Act. I've no control over it and people think it's weird. I am weird. Anyway, I wheeled back in and started to look at the books. There were thousands of them. Most had belonged to some old politician who got fed up with them and gave them to this library so people a hundred years later could read them. God knows why. Then I started to look at them. There was a system to looking at them: you put a slip of paper with the book's name and number in the place where the book had been then you could take it to a desk and read it. When you finished it you took it to the librarian's desk and he would put it back into the proper place. I expect there was a reason for doing it that way. Grown-ups do that sort of thing; it makes them feel secure to have systems that don't make sense to anyone else. It's a tribal thing.

That library excursion was the first of a long series of visits. We did go to the seaside and build castles and fly kites and eat ice cream. We took trips on trains and busses and boats and aeroplanes. Bill seemed to reckon that I had a lot of missed experiences to catch up on. And I went back to school. Not a special school, a normal one. It was called a sixth form college named after some ancient scientist who had discovered Oxygen and the teachers were lecturers and called us by our first names. I don't know why that mattered but it did. I expected a rough time from the other kids, students, sorry, but I didn't get it. I made friends and they came to my house and I went to theirs. We went to coffee shops, legally, and to pubs illegally. We went to festivals and camped overnight in muddy fields and danced to wild music and, just the once, smoked something that messed with my brain and scared the shit out of me. I've never smoked anything since, except trout and salmon which I'd caught myself.

I've just re-read everything I've written so far. When I started to write it was as if I was writing about three different people: first Jodie up to the time her mum died, then Jodie during her adolescence and last of all me, grown up and as I am now. Three people, one of whom I disliked. Adolescent Jodie. I hated writing about her. I considered only devoting a paragraph to her but that would have been wrong. There's more to tell about her and I find that there are parts of her story I like and admire.

That time when she was attacked, raped, in the school boiler room. She fought back, attacked her three attackers and walked back, stark naked to her classroom and took her place at the front of the class. That took some balls. She never complained, refused to name her assailants and wouldn't say a word about what had happened. It just happened that three senior pupils were bleeding badly from scratches to their faces and couldn't explain how they came by such wounds. They left the school and Jodie stayed. Yes, that was me. I'd better stop calling me 'her' or 'she'! I'm proud to be reminded that I played silly chess games with a senior cleric and that a Peace Envoy chatted with me for two hours and persuaded me to try for university and even advised me to study history. I'm proud of the fact that I had the sense to follow her advice instead of automatically rejecting it and drifting into a life of crime. I started to grow up in those first weeks with Sue and Bill. I allowed myself to become part of something I thought had gone forever, a team. A team called a family.

Then there was the trip to Germany. My first flight. Manchester airport at some utterly ungodly hour. Don't they know that adolescents need sleep? Lots of it. It was already a major effort to struggle into school for half past nine every morning. I was allowed thirty minutes grace every morning because of possible problems with taxis. I refused to let mum or dad drive me in. It was my job to be there on time: I was grown up now. Almost. Where was I? Manchester. At six in the morning on a half-term holiday. Terminal Three. Terminal felt right. And we had to suffer a cheerful taxi driver who chatted loudly about his holidays in Africa. Why do they do that?

The wheels proved useful. We got to be first in the 'search for your hidden bomb' line. They found my nail scissors. In my shoulder-bag. Cheek. Would they have nail scissors in Germany? Travel is such a worry. My wheels got us to be first on the plane and the crew were really nice. Naturally we were last to get off the plane. I wasn't sorry because I'd become quite fond of flying. The fight was through a bit of cloud but most of the time I had a good view of the outside world from six miles high. Would it be a poor joke if I said the time flew by? OK. The time flew by. We were met by a nephew of Bill's. He had a camper van too, a bit newer and this one didn't have a name. He also had a German wife and a couple of

teenage boys who were so incredibly polite, all the time, I believed they were taking the Micky, but they weren't. They were just being normal. Boys who thought that being polite was normal? The driver sat on the wrong side and I couldn't find the sliding door until it was pointed out to me. They drove on the wrong side of the road but as everybody else did it didn't seem to matter. It was a bit like the weird game of chess I played with the purple shirt man. Things came at you from the wrong angle. I almost decided to revert to being dumb but didn't. By the time they got to their house, which wasn't a house but a very large flat with a huge living room overlooking a park and a big kitchen diner and four bathrooms and even more bedrooms ... no sliding doors though. The boys even helped to set the table and serve the meal and tidy up afterwards. I realized why we were there: I was being civilised. The wild child from Cheshire was being shown the other side of the coin. I quite liked it. We were there for a week and by the end of it I had been brain washed. I found myself setting the table for dinner and then clearing away and filling the dishwasher. I was laughing and joking with the boys and they weren't raping me. They had girlfriends anyway: a couple of pretty blondes who were also very polite and very funny and spoke excellent English just as well as the boys did. The older boy, Ernst, could drive the camper and the five of us youngsters went out, showing the simple Cheshire lass the River Rhine and on the second excursion we were joined by a very presentable lad, Max, who wasn't in the least horrified by the forty percent of me that wasn't in working order but was quite happy with the sixty per cent that was. I learned why the group called the van the 'Snogmobile'. I enjoyed the week, and waved a sad bye-bye to Max as we left for the airport on the seventh day. I needed a rest too.
'Cheshire cat?' dad said as we settled into our seats before take-off.
'What?'
'You haven't stopped grinning since Tuesday.'
'?'
'Tuesday. The day you met Max. You've grinned ever since.'
'Nah. You're mistaken. Mum said it was about time for your eye-test. Max who, anyway?'
'Max who joined your gang on Tuesday afternoon and spent every daylight hour not more than a metre away from you?'
'Oh, that Max? I wondered who he was. Didn't really notice him.' Don't let anyone tell you that black girls don't blush. I was still grinning as we landed. Text-messaging is wonderful. When I got back to school, sorry, college, on the Monday I could only giggle when asked 'How did the holiday go?' They knew. I had a peer group at last.

It's interesting, this looking back on my life. I know it's self-centred, selfish, ego-wotsical, and why am I wasting my life on something that's dead and gone? Yes, OK. Mum's dead and gone, those foster-parents are dead and gone, and I killed my goldfish with the wrong sort of love. But Max said that all the things that had happened to me had contributed to me becoming me. I wouldn't be the person that I am today if those things, including the rape and the assaults from Paedo Plank hadn't happened. Would I have become an athlete without the accident? Questions like that. We'd talked all night, that last night in Germany. They'd let Max share my room and we'd shared the same bed. I don't know if that was right or wrong, but I'm glad it happened. Of course we explored one another's body, played with the naughty bits, kissed and cuddled and cuddled and kissed, but … but we talked too. I told him everything about me, my thoughts, my thinking about killing myself – you didn't know about that, did you? We talked and we played and it seemed the night would never end. But it did. Of course it did. Max travelled with us to the airport and we had to be dragged apart. Not really, but it felt like that. That's why I was grinning all the way home. I didn't know if I'd ever see him again, perhaps he was like that with any silly slapper he met. But. But he was like that with me. I was a silly slapper, but I was. I was a girl, a female, a young woman, and I'd had a boy in my bed. I felt grown up and childish at the same time. I was the little girl without a worry in the world and love for my mum. I was the stroppy teenager who was bullied and spat on. I was the animal who attacked the kids who were raping me, made them bleed and walked naked in anger. I was the girl who enjoyed being touched in places that the rapists, including the Plank, wanted to touch. Max gave me something that I thought had been stolen from me. Maybe I never would see him again; maybe there never again would be a man in my life, in my bed, in me, in love. In the way that chocolate can replace a bad taste Max had replaced bad memories, had given me something that might change my life. I looked out of the plane's tiny window. Somewhere beneath those beautiful swirling clouds was my friend, my lover, my boyfriend.

Lots of things happen without being noticed. I guess that everybody who wakes up, gets up, washes, has breakfast, goes to work, makes love, listens to music - does all those normal, natural things – goes to bed a slightly different person. We change, slightly, but we do change. After the Plank first touched my bum I changed. He'd started off by showing me pictures of woman and men.

'We could play those games' he said. 'It would be fun' he said. But they weren't games and it wasn't fun. I felt dirty. I felt it was wrong. Mum had never touched me like that. Nobody had. But this man was my foster dad. He said it was OK for him to do these things, he was supposed to: it would help me to grow up. I didn't want to grow up, but he kept telling me I was a big girl now and this was the sort of game big girls played. He said he'd give me nice presents and money if I played the games with him. When my foster mum came home from work he said that we'd had a nice day and that we'd played some nice games and she smiled and said wasn't that nice and I was lucky to have a foster dad who spent nice times with me and liked me so much. So I thought that she must know all about the sort of games he made me play and so it must be all right and there must be something wrong with me. So I stole a bottle of painkillers from the cupboard in the bathroom and when he'd put my bedside light out that night, after he'd kissed me goodnight and said we'd play an even better game tomorrow I swallowed all the pills that were in the bottle. I was dreadfully sick and really thought I was going to die and I was quite glad. But I didn't die. I messed the bed and was very sick again and I fell asleep in my own mess and when she found me next morning she was really cross with me.

'We bought that bed especially for you and you've ruined the mattress. You can sleep on the floor tomorrow night and see how you like that. No school for the rest of the week, see how you like that! You're a stupid wicked evil little monster and you don't deserve a nice home like this. You could have killed yourself. We give you everything a motherless child could wish for and this is how you pay us back.'

They didn't call an ambulance or take me to hospital. Perhaps they were afraid that Social Services would know what had really happened, but I didn't think of that at the time. He left me alone for a few days but then it started again.

I was looking down at the clouds, remembering all this and thinking about Max. Max and I had done all those things, played those same games. But with Max it was OK. It was really fun, and, given the chance, I'd play the same games, and more, again. But it would have to be with somebody I liked and trusted. Somebody, perhaps, I loved. Somebody who loved me. How do you know if somebody really loves you? I stared at the clouds but they didn't tell me the answer.

The fasten you safety belts sign came on and we cruised down through the cloud. Stupidly, for a moment I thought that when we landed I'd see Max again. That was a really stupid idea; he must be a thousand miles away. But it was a nice thought. Dad held my hand. Not that I was nervous, of course but it was only my second landing and it was nice to know he was there. I glanced across and saw that he was holding Mum's hand too. I wondered why they still held hands. They must have been married at least as long as I'd lived. I'd enjoyed holding Max's hand but Mum and Dad were ages old. Why would they still be holding hands? Would Max still be holding my hand in ninety years? Would the nice naughty things we'd been doing still be nice and naughty thirty years from now? Maybe I could ask Mum sometime. Or maybe it was one of those private things you had to keep secret.

We flew in circles round a hilly place. Dad said it was Derbyshire. I kept seeing the same sheep in the same fields. They ignored us. I don't suppose sheep wave to aeroplanes. Maybe they communicate in some other way known only to the Government. Eventually the plane straightened up and we rushed low over the fields and houses until we landed, very gently this time, on wet tarmac at Manchester. It took ages to get off the plane. We were last because of my wheels. We flashed our passports at the Border Guards and went down to collect our bags. Mine felt heavier than I expected but I didn't have time to check it. We went outside and Mum got a taxi for us. I was still looking for Max.

When we reached home I rushed my bag into the bedroom and struggled with the lock. The bloody thing took ages to open. There was a teddy bear inside. A brand new cuddly brown bear with an ear ring. He was holding an envelope. In the envelope was a long letter, nicely written, signed 'with love, Max' and a lot of photographs. And a big box of chocolates. And a packet of condoms with a note – 'maybe next time? Are you busy at Christmas?' I undressed and climbed into bed with the bear and the letter and the photographs and the condoms. I wasn't going to wash his kisses away. Not yet.

Again I wanted to dream but I just fell asleep. I woke up about dawn and watched the room become visible. Bear had fallen out of bed. I had a panic when I couldn't find the letter Max had written. It was crumpled up on the floor underneath Bear's bottom. The photos were scattered about the bed. The one Ernst had taken of Max and me snogging by the river was actually in my hand. Looking at it, like reading the letter, felt a bit like spying on somebody who wasn't me. Intrusive, that's the word. How stupid is that? Me spying on me? Daft.

The civilisation of Jodie rolled on. Because I had such crap exam results – cancel that, no exam results – Sue did a bit of research and discovered a two year course cramming course, run by the local college which would help me get access to a university course. History, I decided, was to be my future. Sorry, joke. I had a long chat with my tutor. She was really good, laid it on the line that I would have to work harder than ever before in my life, offered a lot of support, looked cheerful, was positive I could do it. She knew my own history – my reputation – and mentioned that a couple of my mates were doing the same course and that I could make a great success of it. And that I'd love History.

Me? Make a success? Of books and learning, stuff like that? I didn't ask if she was delusional, but she read my mind.

'Jodie, do you honestly think I would waste my breath setting you up to fail? If I didn't think you could do it I'd suggest you took a different course. You've got a bloody good brain and it's my job to help you realise it.' Shock. Miss swore. Miss said I've got a bloody good brai … brain. Nobody had ever said that to me before. I looked at her.

'Miss, you'd better be bloody right about this or I'll haunt you. You won't dare to go to sleep ever again if I don't make it.'

'Good enough' she said, and smiled. I thought about this on the way home. Me, making teachers smile? I could understand me making teachers swear, I'm sure lots of mine had, when they got home, opened the Gin and swallowed a few glasses. 'God, that Sonko girl's a right little sod' or 'Thank god I don't have to see that little bugger Jodie again till Tuesday.' But smile? Chat to me? Say 'Hi!' when we meet in the supermarket? Now that was weird. The other kids were weird, too. Good weird. They didn't only talk about sex. Well, they did, but not all the time. They talked about sport – I was included because I'd started to win a few wheelchair marathons – music, all sorts of music, and many of them played and sang and two even made their own guitars. They knew about electronics and rainbows and investing money and where to buy the best fish and chips. Two were writing poetry, half a dozen had shares in a racehorse, I was invited to join a group restoring damaged canoes for a children's home and in between all this activity we talked about sex. My point? Well, I was starting to think I was verging on the edge of normality. I wasn't just a black cripple freak; I was one of the gang. When we were out in Warrington one Saturday afternoon a group of yobs from a neighbouring town started making fun of me. It got really nasty and I was scared. The friends I was with saw that I was getting a bit upset and they formed a barrier between me and the yobs. They didn't do anything, just stood there and stared at the trouble makers. Then they started to walk towards them, slowly. The yobs shrugged, yelled a few more insults about cripples then ran. A group of shoppers cheered and jeered as they ran off and congratulated my friends on acting like proper grown-ups. I hadn't noticed any of the grown-ups acting properly, but the thought was there.

It wasn't the only time something similar had happened. There always had been people who objected to my presence on the planet. Sometimes it got really nasty. Once, in a care home, I was given a meal. Bacon, egg, chips and a side helping of dog shit. I assumed it was dog. Some kids would spit in my fruit juice, or throw piss all over my clothes and hair. Names can never hurt me? Don't you believe it: names hurt. Even now, when I'm competing in local events I get comments like 'Of course all the drugs you're on won't show up on tests because they get mixed up with your medication!' 'You Blacks can get away with cheating' and 'I bet she got disabled because she wasn't good enough to win a proper race!'

Medication? Me? I loathe taking tablets. But you can't convince some people. So I just smile and nod and wink. It took me ages to manage to wink but it was worth it just to see the look on their faces. If I get the chance I run over their toes, accidentally of course. Can't help it can I? I'm just a stupid black bitch …Looking at me in the mirror I have to grin. Stupid black bitch grins back at me. I can almost see Rachel looking over her shoulder, smiling as she walks away, fading away, back into the past. There's a reflection of my bed, queen size, and the mirror has reflected a fair amount of action on the bed. On the wall next to the mirror, is a framed copy of my degree. 2.1 in Victorian Studies. Through the window I can see Van, my van, with its own sliding door. My trophy cupboard has a neat collection of medals and cups, nothing gold yet but there's time for that. Not bad for a stupid black bitch I say, and, for a moment, my breath clouds the mirror like a passing ghost. I've been thinking about what Max said, all those years ago, about me becoming the person I am because of what had happened to me. He'd said it as if it was something good, something creative that I should be proud about. On the lines of 'what doesn't kill me makes me stronger'. What would I have grown up like if my dad hadn't run away and mum hadn't died? Would I still have been an athlete, a student, a lover? Would I still have bought a camper van and travelled through Europe, mainly on my own? Would I have met the same boy friends? I probably would never have met Sue and Bill, or Max. I probably would never had had such a horrible car accident, never had spent a night in a care home or with a foster parent. No, I wouldn't have been me. I'd still have been a version of me, black of course. I love being black now, and people who love me I think would love me whatever colour I might be. I hope I'd have been at least a bit bloody minded, have seen injustice clearly, have recognised love, been a bit like the Good Samaritan – though not quite so much of a control freak. People should have choices; and that's what I've had, choices. I got some right (yes, Bill and Sue and your sliding doors – I got that one very right), and other things I got very wrong. I'm me.

Do you ever lie awake at night trying to remember everyone in your life? People who have been important to you and people who didn't seem important at the time but became important later?

S'me again. Guess which silly black bitch is in hospital again? Got it in one. Me. Not proper hospital, A and E. This is the place where idiots with too little brain or too much machismo end up on Saturday nights. Or where SBBs wake up when they try racing Warrington busses with a wheelchair. The wheelchair's fine, since you ask. I knocked myself out for ten minutes so they've imprisoned me in a ward and taken my brains away in a jar to laugh at. They keep asking me what day is it and how many fingers they're holding up. I answer in kind. One nurse tries not to laugh. She's Irish and later that night she sits with me and tells me Irish folk tales about the children of Leah. In return I scare the teeth out of her head by relating a somewhat embellished version of my biography. She said that Max sounds good. For some reason I'm given a dose of apple pie and custard at three o'clock in the morning and Irish said that I have normal responses. I get brain scans and x-rays and all sorts of examinations which are carefully explained to me but which I forget as soon as they're over and done with. I'm discharged with sheets of advice and information and a heart monitor attached to sticky things on my chest with the advice to wear it for a week and hand it back to them before breakfast on the seventh day. They do specify a time but it is long before my breakfast. Bill and Sue and Belinda Two come and collect me and refuse my request to be taken back to my flat. I'm kidnapped. Back to the bungalow and my old room. It's like coming home. It is coming home. I'm invited to stay till I outstay my welcome.
'How long's that going to be?' I ask.
'Anything from five minutes to five years' says Bill.
'I do have a life, you know.'
'And we want it to be a long and happy one' says Sue.
'Right, then. Ten minutes max' I say.
'Max?' says Sue. 'Max who?' If they had a cat I'd throw it at her. They do have a cat but it's a friend of mine. I only throw psychotic cats and there's a scarcity of those in this neighbourhood.
It's a bit like returning to my childhood. I've only been living on my own for a year, and not on my own all that time either. But being home, with mum and dad, is odd. I've seen them most weeks because I'm doing History in the local Uni. We see one another in town, in coffee shops or Marks and Sparks, and we greet and smile and laugh and exchange gossip. But this is different, being under the same roof again. I ache all over and Sue is wonderful. Because I'm condemned to wear the heart monitor for a week I can't bathe or take a shower and Sue sponges down the bits of me it hurts to reach. It's oddly intimate but relaxing. I Skype Max most nights and gangs of my mates from college invade the bungalow and chat and snap me while Bill and Sue stand guard and hand out sandwiches and home brew. The week soon passes and at some ungodly hour on the seventh day I roll back into the hospital and hand in my monitor. The receptionist raises an eyebrow when I refer to it as 'Max my demon lover' and explaining that both Real Max and Demon Max have shared my body, though not at the same time, doesn't improve the situation.
'Not at the same time indeed, Miss, I hope.'
'Alas, no. They never met. They both were aware of my heart beat though Real Max raised it and Demon Max merely measured it …' why don't I know when to shut up. Maybe that gift comes with time and experience. I'd rather come with Max. Shut up, Sonko. Down girl. I was informed that my doctor would be informed of the result of

my tests and I should contact her in seven days, unless it was a matter of urgency and the hospital would contact me directly. They didn't and I'm still here. I look out for other traffic now when I cross roads. Honestly, I do. I look out for other things too. Like the furniture in our house. Until I started this History course I never looked at things properly, thought about who made them, what they were made out of, where they came from. A chair was something you sat on. That was all there was to it. It might collapse when you sat on it, it might end up on a bonfire; you could buy another one in a junk shop or you might just sit on the floor. But we had chairs that were like works of art. Somebody had designed them. I got Bill to tell me about them He looked at me sort of weird when I asked him. But when he saw I was interested he started talking. The chairs round the kitchen table, for instance. Two had come from his Great-grandad's farmhouse in Wales. The ladder-back was from a junk shop in Todmorden. The other three were from a farm sale in Bordeaux. He'd spent weeks scraping the layers of paint until he got back to the natural oak. He said every piece of furniture, every picture, every carpet and every ornament in the bungalow had a history and a connection to either his family or Sue's and now they had a connection to me. I was part of the family. Sue, it seemed, was the clock girl. There was at least one clock in every room. There were three in the living room. One was a big tall thing, in a black wood case. It sometimes struck thirteen and the weight would crash down when you least expected it. It scared the shit out of me when I first came to live here. It had a very slow tick and if I was alone in the room at night I found I was breathing in time to the tick. Breathe in, one, two, three. Hold breath, one, two, three. Breathe out, one, two, three. Hold, one two, three. Breathe in, one, and so on. I made up ghost stories about that clock. It was called a long case clock and it was too easy to imagine that the case had been made from a re-cycled coffin. The two other clocks in the room were scared of the big one and only ticked and tocked very quietly. There was a walnut bureau with secret compartments. Sue said there was a secret for every day of the week and challenged me to find them all. I found five, and Bill said that was as many as he'd managed to find. Sue smiled but she wouldn't tell us about the secrets we couldn't discover. The only clue she gave was that we weren't looking in the right place but we'd guessed that already.

I loved listening to them chatting. They seemed to have a sort of shorthand conversation. They could chat for ages without saying what it was they were actually talking about. It drove me mad. They finished each other's sentences without falling out. I suppose when you've lived with a person for such ages words might become a bit stale and telepathy would creep in without you noticing it. Like I say, it drove me mad. 'You're both bananas' I would say. 'Right, you're right. We're both empty bananas!' Bill would grin. 'Make a good title for a song, Empty Bananas. I'll give you a box of chocolate fish if you can write a song with that title' I never did, but he gave me the chocolates anyway. From Belgium. The fish were scrummy.

There was a big desert of empty time in my life. Post mum and pre sliding doors. I wonder how other people measure their lives. I'd asked Max and he gave his as pre Jodie and post her. I asked where he'd post me to and he said 'First class to my bedroom' and I'd laughed because he thought that was what I wanted to hear but it wasn't. I'd wanted to find something out about him, something private between just the two of us. I suppose I had, that he could be cheap and creepy but he hadn't known that I'd wanted seriousness from him so he'd made a joke of the moment. It made me sad, until he kissed me. I thought I saw something in his eyes, like he was, for a moment, realising that I was something more than a girl who wanted to bed him. It was like a wrong word in a sentence. Then he tickled me and we laughed and the moment was lost. Mum was the only other person who'd tickled me. Bill and Sue treated me respectfully, like I was a serious person who disapproved of frivolity. I'm not. Respect is good, but it shouldn't slide the door to fun shut. I'm getting this wrong: it's like a missing piece of a jigsaw that needs completing. You've got nine hundred and ninety-nine pieces in the right place but the picture is wounded, you only see the missing bit. That's what I am, missing a piece. I'm not complete. A bit is broken, ruined, wounded. I feel complete some days, most days now, since sliding doors came into my life. Lie. Since Bill and his wife came into my life. I'm stuck here in bed and thinking. Look, it's four thirty seven in the morning and I'm examining my life. Why? It's not perfect, but it's perfect for me, as I am. What would make it perfect? Being able to walk and run is the obvious one. Would they have adopted me if I had been in good working order? I asked Sue that, once. She'd stared at me, frowned, 'Yes, of course. We didn't fall for a break in your spine. How could you think that? We fell for you: cheeky, bright, living life, speaking your mind, being you, Jodie. We love you because you are you. I thought you knew that?' I couldn't reply, not at that moment. I just stared at her.

I needed to go somewhere quiet for a while. Just a day or two, to get my head together. I booked into the residential library for two nights. It was the first time I'd ever done anything like that, made a decision about travelling somewhere, making my own arrangements, all on my own. When I finished making the booking I told Bill and Sue what I'd done. They were pleased, thank goodness. Bill asked me if they could come and have lunch with me one day and I liked the sound of that. Bill drove me back to my flat on The Causeway and helped me carry my case to the car park and lifted it into the van for me. He checked I was OK for cash and waved me off on my little adventure.

Automatics are great. I drove past the London Bridge pub on the A49 and turned onto the M56. I was a bit nervous about motorways but the traffic was light and visibility good. I settled into the inside lane at a steady sixty and plodded along for half an hour. It was the first time I'd used the Sat-Nav and apart from the irritating male voice it was quite reassuring. We crossed the River Dee and took the next exit. The big traffic island had traffic lights and from there it was a short drive to the library. Tricky turn into Church Road, lots of parked cars, then we squeezed into the Library car park. I remembered coming here with Sue and Bill, years ago and for a moment I was nervous. I was doing this on my own. I struggled to get my chair out of the van, hoping it wasn't an omen.

It wasn't, unless omens can be good? Who knows? There was a different girl on Reception as I rolled up. She didn't leap up to greet me. Was she being lazy or sensitive? Maybe both. It didn't seem to matter this time. I'd had the sense to book one of the ground floor rooms again. Maybe, one day I'd have access to a room with a view on the top floor, but not today. The room was ready and I showed off a bit, knowing that I knew the way. No Sue this times to unpack my case. 'You're a big girl now.' Who the fuck said that? Nobody there. I knew the voice. 'Rachel? It's you? Why? Thought you'd buggered off?'

'Hi, Jodie. S'me, Rachel. Come to say bye-bye. Hope you'll never need me again, but, if you do …'

'Of course I need you. How can I manage without you? How will you manage without me? How …'

'Jodie, I've been watching you. You set up home without my help; got a lover without my help, bought the Van without … you've grown up, lovely girl. You don't need imaginary friends; you've got some good solid live ones now. Keep an eye on Max.

You look tired, no wonder. Have a lie down on your bed, and I'll become a dream memory for you. Smile when you think of me, smile now …'

She was gone when I woke up. I trundled along to the dining room. Soup, cake and coffee. Just the diet for a grown-up girl. I shared a table with a lady vicar who had just returned from Ghana. She'd been teaching teachers in village schools, polishing their English and Maths. She was mainly interested in Astronomy herself. I quickly sorted that it wasn't astrology and she smiled 'Most people ask why a lady vicar should be interested in telling fortunes by the stars but you didn't even blink!'

I was about to say something witty about not all cripples being thick as … but I didn't.

'I was just thinking that's something else I know nothing about. So, you use a telescope to tell fortunes?' She had the grace to laugh. 'If you're still around later tonight I'll give you a demonstration of what you can see through a scope. It's a bit cloudy now but it's due to clear later, if you're interested? Wrap up warm, it'll be cold later.' Why not? This was the place where I'd played mad chess and decided to study History. Why not give a star a good gaze then?

'Yes, please, I'd like that.'

I've been putting this off. I've rabbited on about doors and wheels and Rachel and God knows what else. It's oddly appropriate that people talk about the elephant in the room because this elephant is about where elephants come from. Africa. Yes, I know they come from India too but the elephant is Africa. I'm African. Well, half of me is. I wonder sometimes which half, the working half or the dormant half. Good things happened in Africa, and something bloody awful happened there too. We'll come to that bit, if I can face it, later. Preferably very much later, like never. We'll see.

I was telling you about my solo trip to that library and about intending to look at stars after dinner. I did intend to, honest. But dinner came first and I came first to dinner. The dining hall was empty when I arrived. Perhaps they should have banged a dinner gong or rung a bell or just shouted 'Come and get it!' But they didn't. I collected my starter, soup, some sort of veggie stuff. I transferred it to my tray, rolled on to give Denise my room number so she could add it to my bill, collected a glass of wine, cutlery, and drew up to a table. All on my own. 'Hello, Jodie! Mind if I join you?' Where had she come from? Silly question. From Africa; she'd told me that the first time we met, years ago. Me, freshly adopted, her, writing a speech.

'Sirra? How did the speech go?' She sat down in the place facing me. 'Fancy you remembering that! It was my first speech in my new job. Nearly lost me the job too. I suppose they'd chosen a Black woman in the expectation I'd sit quietly in a corner with my mouth shut. They should have checked with my dad first!' I looked at her, trying to see the wild child beneath the cloak of adult dignity. She was grinning at me.

'Come to Africa' she said. I'd hoped, for a moment, that common sense would kick in with forty seven sound reasons why I couldn't possibly do such a silly thing. I was a student, I was a traffic hazard, I was … I was longing to go to Africa. Maybe my dad would meet me off the plane and kill me? Maybe a mosquito would drink my blood and leave my corpse for vultures to devour, if crocodiles didn't get me first. Maybe, maybe, maybe.

'Yes' I said.

'No rush, Jodie. Africa can wait a bit longer. It's been there for thousands of years, it can wait. But can you? Take your degree, win some races, go on holiday with your friends. But come to Africa, some time.'

How the fuck did this woman know about my plans for Uni? About the races? About my friends? Obvious, really. Sirra was a friend of my mum and dad. Mums and dads talk to their friends about their children. Maybe all the talk hadn't been about what a pain in the arse their adopted daughter was? Maybe, just maybe, they had been just a tiny bit proud of her getting to college, being offered a place at Uni to study History, maybe a bit interested in her joining the college sports club and entering half marathons? Maybe? I'd kill them. Is nothing private these days? Meanwhile we were chatting about Africa, and about West Africa in particular. I liked the sound of it. The beaches could be a bit of a problem for a wheelchair, I thought. But it seemed that there were some good roads, some good, friendly hotels with lots of downstairs rooms and swimming pools. Sirra mentioned one where her late husband used to stay, a sort of backpackers Hilton, she said. Lots of charity workers and volunteers stayed there. It was named after a tree I'd never heard of. Yes, there were crocodiles and there was at least one pool where you could visit them. Hippos were very dangerous and could bite you in half. Note to self: avoid hippos even if they smile at you. Mosquitoes could kill you.

It seemed that there was a system that travellers could use. You went to a village and gave a present to the chief, she used a different word but it meant chief. You gave the chief a small present, rice, candles, money, and the chief would find you a bed for the night in one of the village houses, you'd also get a meal and you gave your host another small present as a thank you. I couldn't see myself being cheeky enough to ever use it, but you never know.

Some other people joined us. They seemed to know Sirra and after we'd finished the meal, including the excellent bread and butter pudding with ice cream we all moved into the big sitting room, the one with two fireplaces, and drank coffee. The lady who had offered me the use of her telescope joined us and didn't appear to be upset by my having ignored her offer.

'Too cloudy anyway to see much, may be better tomorrow night.' I still felt bad for not having apologised or gone to join her. Note: am I growing a conscience? That'll be a nuisance. We sat up till two o'clock before I made my excuses and rolled off to bed. I'd have to develop stronger stamina if I was to make the grade as a student. Again I intended to lie awake and think about Africa and all I'd learned. Failed again. Head hits pillow, brain goes on strike. The noises of people heading for breakfast woke me next morning. I had a slight shower, damped myself all over and pretended I was clean, dressed in yesterday's clothes – at least I knew where they were – and headed out for food. I was quite pleased that my room was the nearest to food and drink. Lots of people smiled, said 'Good morning' and didn't treat me like a cripple. One did hold a door open for me, an old gent who looked about a hundred and eighty, but I was so out of character that I said 'Thank you, very kind' and gave him the best smile I could manage at that hour of the morning. He smiled back and held the door for somebody else.

Breakfast was croissants and coffee, three cups, and I was raring to go. I went for a roll round the garden while waiting for the library to open for the day. There's a life-sized statue of a lady in the back garden, Sophie, Sofia, some such name. She's a goddess of wisdom or cleverness or books so I suppose she's almost in the right place. Pity she has to stand out in the rain and snow but she may not be a Christian Goddess – do they have any? She looked cold and lonely. I said 'Good morning' to her and rolled off to form a queue of one outside the library. I didn't have to wait long before a young girl with glasses and the key came along and let me in. There were several desks and I picked the one in the middle of the room and plugged my laptop in. I had to crawl under the table to do it but it was nice and clean down there and the wood block floor shone in the morning sun. I hoisted myself back into my chair, fired up the computer and started my research for the day. Gambia. I was going to find out all I could from the internet and check it out with Sirra. Well, I'm a student. We don't believe everything we're told.

It's a country so small it doesn't show up on some maps. It's short and narrow, alternately hot and wet and just hot. There are half a dozen different tribes but they get along with each other. It's a Muslim country and they don't just say 'hello' when they meet but ask 'Is there peace?' and answer 'There is only peace' which I thought was nice. We English used to rule it but now they have their own democracy and a President with a big smile. English is still the common language because it's spoken in the schools so that should make visiting easier. Sirra speaks English so well you wouldn't think she was a foreigner. I thought back to the kids in one of my schools who'd chanted 'Monkey girl, monkey girl, get back to Africa and climb a tree' at me. Well, maybe I would do just that. Apart from the tree, of course. I missed lunch because I was so busy working. I found lots of info: languages, legends, place names, advice on dress and what to pack and flights and so many things. When you stay in that library you can just leave your things on your desk and nobody will touch them. About five o'clock I did just that and rolled along to my room for a freshen up. By the time I'd freshed it was dinner time. I joined a queue and took my place at one of the small tables for four. Sirra came and joined me and the telescope lady and a friend of hers ate with us.

'Well?' said Sirra. I told her what I'd found out and that I was going to look for pictures and maps after dinner. I was so tempted by the thought of going exploring. After all, my dad, whoever he was, had made the journey, there to here and back again. Was I going to look for him? I didn't know the answer to that. I finished my pudding, jam roly-poly and custard, and headed back to my desk in the library. I was the only person in there and it felt special. Built so long ago, visited by famous people from all over the world, and here's me, SBB, with the place all to myself, and the people in charge trust me to behave decently, not to steal books or throw them around or scribble all over the pages. Me. Trusted. SBB treated as a human. Treated as a human and encouraged to travel on a journey to find her people. That sounded dead pretentious. I thought of my mum, my birth mother, seduced by a charmer, ignored by her blood relations, devoted to me, trying to make my life exciting and fun. She would have loved this place and its people. She would have longed for the chance to plan a journey like mine; perhaps she had imagined travelling with my dad, walking through hot sand at the edge of a blue sea. She deserved it, deserved to live her dreams. Are you allowed to cry in libraries? I sobbed, quietly, as I remembered the last time I saw her alive. I had to do it for her, to make the journey she would have rejoiced in making. I dried my tears, blew my snotty nose, and settled back to work.

As I worked I was thinking with the spare brain cells about the practicality of making the journey. I was fortunate; I had the cash to spare. It felt odd, sitting there, alone as darkness fell and only the shaded lamps of the old building fended off the gloom, me planning a journey to another continent. Of course zillions of people travel, but this was my journey. My adventure. Would I even be allowed to travel by myself? Wouldn't airlines demand I take a carer along too? Did I really need this? I'd driven myself about for ages, visited Scotland and London under my own steam, but Africa? A step too far for someone who can't walk? Time for more research. Google …

I needed the loo. It would be at the far end of the long corridor which ran from the door to the library, past the reception office, past the dining room and cakes, up to the door to the common room with two fireplaces. Just before the door to the common room you wheel sharp right and the loos are on your right. It was twice the distance to my room but, hey, I'm a student and we use the student loo. I was on my way back from the loo that a thought occurred to me. Are there loos in The Gambia? Do sub-Saharan countries have flush loos? Taps, do they have taps? How do people on wheels manage if they don't? Now there's a subject for research. Sirra must know. But she's an elder stateswoman sort of person. She also was, and I'd checked, a cover girl for some fashion magazine so posh I'd never heard of it. But I'd seen some of the shots and there was no doubting it. And she'd written books. Until a couple of years ago I'd barely read a book. She had a string of letters after her name that reached across a page. I couldn't ask her how to go to the loo in her village. Can you imagine asking an almost complete stranger, a person at least as important as the Prime Minister, how to use a loo? And if I couldn't find that out I just couldn't go anywhere. Bugger. Sh- no, better not use that word. I could be properly p… off. Sorry. Stupid idea anyway. Why bother to go to a country so small it's not on most maps but it should be with a big warning notice about the loos. Or lack of them. Forget it. College was much safer.

Somehow I found the words to tell Sirra that I had decided to concentrate on my studies before I started touring the world. I was surprised and a bit disappointed at the ease with which the words came to my lips. Maybe I should have crossed my fingers behind my back as the lies tumbled out. That had worked fairly well when I was a child but it was me I was lying to now as well as Sirra. She was smiling and nodding as I spoke, telling me I was being very grownup and sensible and I knew she was fibbing as much as I was, She wanted me to travel and see her village and I was letting a lavatory come between us. I'm a lying coward and I felt she was looking into my soul as I lied. Bill and Sue were due to arrive for their posh afternoon tea, and I invited Sirra to join us. We sat round one of the dining tables, properly posh with a white table cloth and china teacups with saucers and a milk jug. I would have said 'just like home' but it was posher than home. Bill took our pictures but I wasn't sure I wanted to be reminded of the day when I had chickened out of an adventure. It was all very friendly but there was no sparkle. My Gambian research seemed a bit pointless too. When the elders had finished the last dainty sandwich and I'd licked up all the crumbs, not really, what do you think I am? They all left and I went for a trundle round the village. I only got as far as the village shop because I met mister purple shirt who asked if I'd invented any new varieties of chess and I lied to him as well and invited him to a pawn-less battle. Even though he was a priest of some sort he seemed willing to set aside established rules. I began to take him seriously and we played the game by firelight late that night. I'd never had much to do with priests, apart from the guy who prayed me into my first operation after the car crash. Purple shirt was OK though.

Ah, I'd forgotten another priest. I've only had his word that he was a priest, this chap I'm thinking about. A few months ago, when Van was being awkward and refusing to start one cold morning I decided to get a bus to college. I wrapped up in everything that would go on me and trundled out to the bus stop. I'd heard that wheelchairs could get onto buses so, here we go, I thought. Not with the first two buses that come along we didn't.

'Sorry, love, can't get the ramp down'. Bugger. I was getting colder when the idiot came along. I heard him first, reciting a poem about his lord being a shepherd and going for a swim. He was a fattish bloke, bald, wearing a T-shirt, shorts and trainers. And singing. Fortunately, he stopped singing.

'Hiya, sister. The Lord is with you.' Humour him. He's mad. Keep calm and the cold will kill him presently. Presently means very soon and that will be a present to me. He can't harm me, keep calm. I'm wrapped up like a pass the parcel parcel.

'Good morning, my Lord.' Humour him, but don't smile. He'll think I'm laughing at him and he'll kill me.

'Good morning, sister. It's a lovely day, isn't it?'

'Almost a lovely, but it's cold enough to freeze the …' Help, he's a priest, or he thinks he is. No blasphemy. '…cold enough to freeze the ducks on the canal.' Phew. I ducked out of that in time! 'Aren't you cold?'

'No, of course not, sister. The Lord's love protects me from all harm Will you pray with me?' and he went down on his knees by my side. Fortunately I wasn't required to give consent or to join in. He prayed loud and as embarrassingly long as a missionary about to be eaten might have done. A bus drew up and the driver flipped down a ramp and manhandles me into the bus. Into the warm, quiet bus where people decided not to see me or speak to me. Just as I wanted it. Warm, quiet, bliss. I was almost on time for college. The mad priest overtook the bus at Bridge Foot. The traffic always gets caught there. He had a fair turn of speed though. I had difficulty concentrating during lessons. I kept looking out of the window to check that the priest wasn't about to burst into hymn singing or serenading or preaching or whatever else noise priests make. If he was a priest. If he'd called me "sister" one more time I'd have brained him. It did make me think again about not having any brothers or sisters though. One of them might have turned out like him. Maybe that would be OK, what with being related to you and you having known him or her all your life. Though you might have hoped they would grow up and become car mechanics or hairdressers or travel agents or …, or anything other than publicly praying priests. Or politicians. Or professional care workers. Sorry, that's not fair. I'm rambling again. I wish I really could go rambling, running round hills and lakes and canals like I used to do. That was good. I'm being mean. I've had loads of fun since I've been in a chair. I've had a boyfriend and I've been dancing and racing and out to discos and I've learned to drive and I can travel on a bus and I can go quarter of the way down an escalator and I'll probably live long enough to do loads of daft and crazy things like get married and have babies and travel to meet people of my own race. I might even find out if I am a Mandinka girl like Sirra thinks I might be. If I stop fannying around and get my act together.

Classes ended. Should I call them lectures? I'm a college girl, not a school girl. School girls have lessons. School girls probably run screaming from publicly praying people. How should I know?

'Jodie! Are you coming or not?'

'What, where?'

'To the pub. You can get us in. You look like a proper bag lady. The Rambling Fern will serve you.'

'I could get locked up.'

'No chance. You had a blessing this morning. Bomb proof. Spritzers all round. Here's the money. We'll be in the lounge with the other drunks. Hank will help you.'

'What if they won't serve me?'

'They've got to. It's discrimination if they don't. Sue them. You've got the money.'

I get talked into things. Do they have easy access cells in prisons? Would I have to be carried everywhere by a multiple mass murderer? Do they have mixed prisons? I bet they'd discourage wheelchair marathons. Did I tell you I'd won a couple? Me two, Hank three. I'll get him yet. Spike his drink with peppermint. That'll fix him. This lot are looking at me, grinning. They'll start chanting in a minute. I hate it when they do that. "Jodie for Queen, Jodie for Queen. Vote for Jodie, Jodie for Queen. Jodie the secret black racing machine." Nonsense,

And procedurally unsound. Queens get born to the job. Still, a Black T10 sex mad queen? Could be fun.

Why am I telling you all this? Students go for a drink. Hardly newsworthy. But it is. This is me, Jodie no-friends, the stupid black bitch. SBB girl. With friends. Friends who call round at our house, friends who buy me nice silly things for my birthday, who take me dancing, who turn out on bloody cold days to cheer me on when I'm racing. No, I'm not going to cry.

'Come on, Hank. Carry the drinks, mate.'

I didn't tell you about the piece of stone, did I? I'd forgotten about it in the kerfuffle with the priest and travelling by bus and getting a little drunk in the Rambling Fern pub. Nothing too bad, we didn't get thrown out but on my way to the bus stop, all of fifty metres from the front door of the pub, I wove a wobbly course. So I forgot about the stone until I found it at the bottom of my rucksack. Sirra had handed it to me as I left the library to head for home.

'Jodie, here you are: find out about this bit of flint. You like research? It should tell you something about your people.' People? My people? Bill and Sue? Hank and Max? My long departed dad? Who?' I dropped the thing into my bag. I was more worried about getting on to the motorway and coping with the traffic. Easy to forget, a bit of stone. But there it was, tipped out on the spare bed with my dirty washing and notebook and other odds and ends. I was still shaking. Some idiot in a flash car had picked on me to play silly buggers with on the motorway. I'd noticed him tailgating me for a few miles then he pulled out and drove alongside for a while. When I slowed, he slowed. When I speeded up a bit, he speeded up. Then he dropped back and tailed me for a few miles then suddenly overtook me, pulled sharply in front and braked hard. I just managed to brake hard enough to avoid ramming him and he speeded up a bit. He repeated this splendid, intelligent game a couple of times. What fun we had. Not. He tailed me off the motorway onto the A49 and obviously wanted to follow me home. I drove into Stockton Heath and stopped outside the police station in the middle of the village. He was so thick he didn't see the 'POLICE' sign outside. He got out and walked up to Van, tried to open the door. I sounded the horn, and kept my hand on it. A couple of women in uniform walked out and saw my problem. Idiot tried to make a run for his car but one woman tripped him up. The other came to chat to me. She invited me in for a cuppa tea. I was shaking, so I didn't make a fuss when she helped me get into my wheelchair. She pushed me into a room that might have benefitted from an interior decorator's touch, but the tea and biscuits left nothing to be desired.

'You OK now? You're Jodie Sonko, the athlete, aren't you? Some of our lads have seen you out training, very early some mornings. You've got a fair turn of speed. Hope you don't mind them keeping an eye out for you?' I giggled. Nerves, just nerves. Nerves plus the image of a herd of police men popping their glass eyes into the shopping bag strapped to the back of my trike, then groping about like zombies to find their patrol cars. Nerves, just nerves. There was a commotion outside the door.

'I'll fucking kill that black crippled bitch. Let me get me hands round 'er throat. I'll make her see sense ...Ow!'

'Oh, dear, he's fallen over again. Don't worry about him, Miss Sonko. We'll get him the treatment he needs... .' I hoped it would involve a lot of walking until he got his licence back.

'Do you need me to give evidence?'

'Possibly. But there's loads of CCTV, and other people have complained about him. A couple of our lads were following you along the motorway and they filmed his activities. And we heard what he called you. If he's any sense he'll hold his hand up and not be any further bother to you.' A knock on the door.

'Inspector Hawk would like a word with Miss Sonko, if you've finished here, Jan?'

Jan had, so we trundled off to be inspected.

The inspector was a fit looking bloke, built like a distance runner. We chatted about running, my mum, my adoption, my college work and my racing. We got through another pot of tea and another plate of biscuits. Chocolate, this time. And he handed over a letter.

'Glad we've seen you, Miss Sonko. You're quite a star. The lads have made a collection for you, to cover a bit of your training expenses. There's an excellent Gym at HQ, and you'll be welcome there too. We've a couple of training experts on staff who would like to help you keep fit. They could make a training programme out for you, if you like. That's if your image could stand being seen with some of our officers now and again?' Bloody 'effin' hell. I don't swear. Course I don't. And I don't dissolve into tears. Never. But I do nick the last biscuit, especially if it's one of those with jam and sponge … Inspector chap grinned, shook my hand, the one not busy with the biscuit, and handed me back to Jan.

Jan saw me safely home, complemented me on my parking skills, and polished off my supply of biscuits and two cups of real coffee made in the coffee pot thing Sue had given me as a moving in present.

I was going to tell you about that piece of stone? Another time. Time for bed now. Been a hell of a day. The cheque? It was made out to me for a hundred and twenty seven pounds forty one pence. I wondered who had given the forty one pence.

The 'phone woke me. Dad Bill having bright ideas for daughters who live on their own. It was the wrong time for waking up on a Saturday morning. There isn't a good time for waking up on Saturdays. Saturday mornings are officially night time. Everybody know that.

'Put the coffee on. I'm on my way round. I've had an idea.' Dads aren't supposed to have bright ideas. They should wait quietly on stand-by, waiting to be called on. Reactive. Proactive dads can cause problems, like calling too early on mornings that are really night times in disguise. I hauled some clothes on. They had lain quietly where they had landed when I discarded them the night before. I'm a student. We're programmed to be scruffy. Even if police people had sort of adopted them. I abluted a bit and managed to have the coffee on before Dad arrived. He does cheerful in mornings. Still, he'd brought fresh croissants from the deli in the village.

'Your Mum's off on one of her jaunts with the Ramblers so I thought we could spend the day annoying one another?'

'You do know it's the middle of the night?'

'There's a bright light in the sky.'

'It's the moon.'

'Say, what light on yonder window breaks? It is the moon, and Jodie is the sun!'

'That's not a yonder window. It's a kitchen window. And I haven't got a lover called Romeo. He's called …'

'Too much information, daughter. Pour the coffee.'

'You pour it, you're nearer to the pot.'

'But I'm a guest. And I'm your respected dad. And pouring me a mug of coffee will improve your social skills so when Romeo does arrive in your life you'll be skilled up ready to deal with him.' I poured.

He picked up the stone from where I'd dumped it on the bread board. He frowned at me.

'What?'

'It's in the wrong place. It's not a knife.'

'?'

'It's a scraper. Look.' He tipped it onto one side. The random looking edge where several chips of stone had been removed lay straight on the wood. I stared at it.

'So what?'

'So somebody designed it like that.'

'Somebody designed a stone?'

'Flint. It's flint. It's a Stone Age tool.'

'I thought they just did arrow heads and axes?'

'And sickles and knives and scrapers.' One side of the thing had obviously been worked on. The edge was still quite sharp and the other side was just natural stone shape. 'He was a bit lazy, this tool-maker. Look, he's not touched this side or this edge.'

'Clever, isn't it? Pick it up.' I picked it up, thinking about what I was doing. It fitted neatly into my right hand, my thumb fitted neatly against a small ridge, and my fore finger curled comfortably round one long edge. Holding it like that brought the cutting edge level with the table top. A small sticky-out point was just beyond the tip of my fore-finger.

'So, what do you know about the girl who used it?'

'What?'

'Look how well your hand fits round it. So, she had hands about your size. She was right-handed, just like you. She may not have been able to run like you used to do.'

'?'

'It's a scraper. It was probably used to clean animal skins. She could have done that sitting down.' I felt a shiver down my spine. Suddenly, she was a real person, this Stone Age girl. A girl about my size, possibly injured, unable to walk, but still able to work for her community, enabled by a small piece of flint. I looked at Dad.

'You're not making this up, are you? I'll hate you if you did.'

'Google, Wiki, and a very helpful lady in the Museum. It's flint, probably from Thetford, in Norfolk. Sorry, I got carried away. I've brought you some post.' Half a dozen envelopes; insurance due for the Van, a couple of begging letters from charities, some bumf from the gym, and an airmail letter from Germany. Max's address on the back. Dad frowning at me. He started to say something, then clammed up.

'Open it, Jodie. You need to.' Of course I need to, it's from Max. Of course it was;

"*Dear Jodie,*

I had a lovely time with you. I want you to know that I'll always admire and respect you. I think you should know that Marlene and I are now engaged to be married. I think that you should also know that I made out with you because some of my friends bet me 50 Euros that I would not take a crippled girl to bed. We had a nice time, I think? No hard feelings I hope. My parents are going to invite your parents to our wedding but I will understand if you do not wish to attend.

Best wishes for the future,

You are a very special girl,

I hope you find a nice guy who doesn't care that you are a cripple,

Max."

Somehow I made it into college the next day. I hated everybody. I hated all males. I hated all females who had males. I hated all children because they were going to grow up and be male similar to the above or be girls who would be similar to the above even though I would warn them. I was debating whether or not to hate mum and dad for the same reasons. They should at least have known and warned me.

'Jodie!' Somebody was calling to me across the yard. Katie Burrows. A girl. A girl with a boyfriend. Sucker.

'What?'

'Have you heard the news this morning, Jode?' I hate it when people mess with my name.

'What?'

'About people, people with spines …'

'People have spines. So do hedgehogs. Worms don't. You think I'm stupid?'

'No. I know you're not. On the news this morning … can we go inside and get a coffee? I'm freezing my balls off out here?'

'You haven't got any balls.'

'Exactly, they dropped off when it started freezing. Come on. It's dead exciting.'

We trundled in. The cafeteria was warm and, oddly, almost deserted. Kate brought coffee and KitKats to our table. Maybe she wasn't such a pain.

'Thanks. What's exciting?'

'The news. I thought you might have heard it. Your mum and dad are intellectuals, aren't they?' I might have to kill her. More chocolate for me.

'Intellectuals? No. Why?'

'I've heard Radio 4 on in your house.'

'Only in the kitchen. That doesn't count.'

'It does. Especially in the kitchen. Radio 4 News. This morning. A mouse can walk.' I will have to kill her. My heart is breaking and she's rabbiting on about mice. Could be worse; she might be rabbiting on about rabbits. Or hares.

'Yes?'

'There's a point to this? I've known that mice can walk. I've seen them do it, in my first mum's kitchen. They can run bloody fast too. They can probably ride tricycles and fly paper planes …'

'Not when their backs are broken.'

'What?'

'Not when their backs are broken. Monkeys, too, with spinal injuries. They can walk a bit too.'

'Katie, you're raving. Sit down. Oh, you are sitting down. I forget what short arse you are. Give me your biscuit, it's wasted on you.'

'Jodie, listen. Some scientists, here in our Uni, have done work on vertebrates with spinal injuries, something to do with electrical impulses, to get legs working again. It's fantastic! Don't you see? They might be able to get it to work on humans. On you!' And old people might live for ever and elephants might juggle ostrich eggs and there might be peace in the world …

'Jodes, listen. It's true. I heard it. In our own Uni, spinal repairs. Why don't you ring them? Offer to be a volunteer, a human labrat. It might work. Imagine life without wheels? Well, you could keep van, I suppose. You might be able to run again. You were talking about a wheelchair marathon? You could do a real marathon, on foot, like proper athletes!' I will kill her. Any minute now I will leap out of this chair and strangle her with her own long, blonde, blonde hair. I'll conceal her body in a bin sack; they'll have stacks of them behind the counter for when they have another disaster like the tiramisu without sugar. I'll chop her up and dump her in the River Mersey to kill the salmon.

'Jodie, have I upset you? How? I'm sorry. We're friends still, aren't we? I thought you'd be pleased. Sorry. What's wrong?'

'Katie, I am an athlete, a proper athlete. I do not have this fucking chair because I'm a lazy idle cunt who can't be bothered to stand up and walk. I've just been dumped by a boy I dreamed might marry me. Turns out he's going to marry, and I quote, a proper girl whose bits work properly and he only fucked me because three of his friends dared him to have it off with a cripple. Yes, Katie, I am upset. I'm upset and jealous that you can walk and run and that normal boys want you in bed because you're beautiful and sexy and clever and funny. I'm jealous that you can walk to the counter and buy a couple of cups of this disgusting coffee and carry them back without breaking anything. I'm jealous because people, nice people, don't look at you with pity, and if they smile at you it's because you're pretty and friendly and you smile at them. If they smile at me I can see that they think I'm a cripple and I'm being brave but they wish I'd get the hell out of their way and out of their sight. Yes, I'll ring the bloody lab but I already know what they'll say because I've heard it a dozen times before. "Thanks for your interest, Miss Sonko. It's a work in progress and shouldn't have been leaked to the press. If there is any real progress that might be applicable to your case you'll hear from your consultant or G.P."

'Sorry, Jodes. Sorry. What can I say?'

'Try putting your brain into gear before engaging your mouth. Think. I love you, I like our friendship but think for a moment how what you say might be interpreted. I am living with a disability. I am not disabled: I think like you, I lust like you, I dream like you and I work bloody hard to share the same courses as you. I enjoy your friendship and if I didn't I wouldn't still be here talking to you. I can't take you on with a running marathon but if you like I'll find you a loan of a proper racing chair and you can see for yourself how difficult it is to do twenty-six and a bit miles on three wheels. If you can keep up with me for half the distance I'll be amazed.'

'Jodie, whoa! That's like me asking you to try running a half marathon from scratch. Tell you what, find me a decent self-propelled chair, not a racing one, and I'll spend next Saturday going round town with you, and going for a night out afterwards. How's that?' I thought about it for a few moments. Annoying though it was, she was right. Maybe more people should try it.

'Fair enough, Katie. You're on. I'll treat you to a meal at the Bridge if you last the day. Ten o'clock start from mine? Wheel into town, morning coffee, shopping, visit the museum, afternoon tea, trip on a bus, your choice, back to mine to freshen up then along the road to The Bridge?'

'I know I'll regret this. Yes, you're on. Ten on Saturday morning at yours. Now get the coffee. Equality of opportunity? Your turn, I think.'

I'm rabbiting on again. I'm avoiding that African elephant. Yes, we did have a day out together. Yes, it was a partial success. Yes we did have a good pub meal at The Bridge. And bloody yes, Katie did pull a really nice guy at the pub when she ran over his foot and knocked a pint out of his hand. So far as I know they're still together. Bugger! Back to the elephant …

There are no elephants in The Gambia. Not wild ones anyway. How do I know? I looked. Yes, I did go. No, my biological father was not waiting at the airport to kill me. Sirra met me at the airport and introduced me to Ed, her husband

I was rocketed through customs and immigration control and my baggage was found and brought out to the car for me. Royalty probably get used to this sort of treatment but it was a novelty for me. God, it was hot. Heat surrounded me like a wall. I'll never complain about the weather in Warrington again. Well, of course I will, but I won't mean it. It's just something people in Warrington talk about. All the time. I bet they do in Widnes and Crewe and Windsor Castle too. Sorry, heat must be rotting my brain cell.

'How was Africa, Jodes?'

'Hot.' Sparkling conversation. Nothing else left to say. Just hot. Africa is hot. And sweaty. And dusty. And bloody wonderful. I am African. My skin has found its true home. I have found me. I am normal here.

Sirra lives in a lovely house. Because she's rich, and her husband is rich, they have electricity and running water and air conditioning. They have two almost new Mercedes 4x4s parked in their compound, his and hers. There's a swimming pool. A Jacuzzi, a fitted kitchen, a everything luxurious you can think of. I bet there's a yacht moored on the river and maybe a private aeroplane in a hangar at the airport. If there is I bet Sirra can pilot it.

They also support several nursery schools, paid for the buildings, trained the staff (and pay them well), and admit children to the schools without payment of school fees, something rare in this country. Sirra and Ed would be a success story in any community in any country in the world. I'm proud to know them. They let me stay with them for three weeks. I learned how to cook Gambian food, and Ed taught me to make Atayah. That's green Gunpowder tea which is served whenever there's an excuse to drink tea. It's cooked in a small enamel teapot: equal measures of tea, water, sugar and mint leaves. It's a complete ceremony, and you can tell immediately who is the most important person present because that person is offered the first drink.

You were going to ask me about lavatories, weren't you? Actually, I managed very well. Ed and Sirra have European style bathrooms, one for each bedroom. All the hotels I visited had them too, so I'd been worried about nothing, at least on that first trip. This sounds like hero worship? Yes, because it is. I'd met good people before, course I had. First mum, Sue and Bill. I'd thought Max was too but hey, I'm human, I can be wrong. Totally wrong. But I'm normal. I'm in my homeland.

I didn't see much of Ed on that first trip. He was away, upcountry, near Basse,supervising the rebuilding of a school. Ten years ago an English couple had offered to build and equip an infant school for a village but had been very keen to get much of the work done for free. They hadn't been willing to pay for cement to make bricks so the bricks were very poor quality. Everybody, including Sirra, had warned them that heavy rain would destroy the walls but the couple were very suspicious about advice given to them by natives so, as predicted, the school fell down. The couple had refused to believe what had happened and were sure that the villagers were determined to cheat them out of more money and would give no further assistance. Sirra and Ed didn't want the school to fail so they stepped in to help with the rebuilding. Ed was living with the Head Master and his family until the school was completed. He did travel home at weekends and we had lots to talk about because before he'd moved out to live in Gambia his home had been near Chester, just a few miles from Warrington.

'Jodie?'

'Sirra?'

'I see that your wheels stick in the sand too much. Would you be insulted if I drive you to meet some of my friends?'

'That would be very kind.' Oh lordy. I've been civilised and I didn't really notice it happening. I sound polite even to myself. She is, of course, a good driver. Is there anything this woman cannot do? She's black, beautiful, educated, more civilised than I'm ever going to be and she's just too bloody nice. I should hate her but I can't. We drive to the next village. Turns out it's not the next village, it's the same one but the rains have washed away the road so we take the long way round. The very long way. As we go we pick up four people, two hens and a goat. They are all, well, the people at least, related to Sirra. We have extended greetings. Sirra is anxious that I learn enough of the tribal language to greet people respectfully. She speaks six languages fluently: English, French, Mandinka, Wolof, Fula and Serehula. I think that's what they all are. Thankfully English is the official language but everyone has their tribal language too. French? The country of Senegal surrounds Gambia on three sides and their official language is French …

We stop in a family compound. There are two long rows of terraced houses; all roofed with corrugated iron, single story whitewashed mud brick walls. There are large trees, mangoes, at the ends of each row and under the trees the women sit on benches, talking and laughing and watching the children and chickens skittering about in the sand. They stare at me. One of the older women speaks. Sirra whispers 'She is greeting you. Remember what I told you to say' I try to remember and mumble something. The old lady smiles and claps her hands. The others smile and laugh, not unkindly. I know what unkind laughter sounds like. Sirra lifts my chair out of the car and settles me into it. My audience stares, silent for a moment, then, as I laboriously wheel through the deep sand to towards them and the shade they start to talk loudly, asking me questions I do not yet understand.

Sirra translates: they are admiring the wheelchair, they marvel at the ease (!) I can travel through the sand. They like the shopping basket hanging from the back of the seat but think it should have a sturdy lock to prevent theft. Why do I have to push the wheels round myself, do I not have family to push me along? Am I too poor to pay for help? Would it not be good charity to employ a man to push me?

I ask Sirra to explain that I am young and that propelling the chair is my exercise. I ask her to mention that I race other people, men and women, over long distances. I also play football in a college team against other teams from other clubs. There is what sounds like a bitter argument but Sirra tells me 'that is not the way here. Un married girls do not play mixed sports, and it is disrespectful because if a girl happens to beat a boy in a race he will not be respected by his friends.' I am about to say something very very rude but fortunately I remember my manners. I mumble something about different tribes have different customs. My audience nods, that must be the reason; not all tribes are as civilised as the Mandinka. Green tea has been brewed and I am offered the first glass. I smile and pass it to Sirra, who accepts it. My audience smile and nod. I feel I have just passed a test. I'm invited into one of the houses to rest. I accept, not because I'm tired but because I'm nosey.

There are two small dark, cool rooms. The front room has two broken wooden chairs and two old plastic garden chairs. There are two metal framed beds in the back room. Eight people live here. Out through the back door is an open air kitchen. A teenage girl is frying fish and adding things I don't recognise to make a sauce. It smells wonderful. Over to the right hand side of the yard is a small fenced area. It's the shower room. I ask about the toilet and the girl points off to another fenced area, a few hundred metres from the house. I decide not to investigate. Open air showers and open air loos. I'm learning. Back in the house the woman indicates that I should lie down for a rest until dinner is ready. Sign language is international. I hoist myself out of the chair onto the bed. She picks up the chair to move it out of the way and is amazed by its lack of weight. She calls to her friends and they all troop in and pick it up in turn. The smile and nod and pat it. The chair is a hit. A mosquito net is draped over me. I try to protest but fingers are shaken and I guess I should do as I'm told. There are holes in the net a bat could fly through, but it's the thought that counts. I am offered protection. Sirra whispers that I will be called in time to wash before lunch, and I am left to it. I'm a half African girl in a totally African setting. The bed is almost comfortable. There's a babble of sounds, women talking, chickens clucking, children singing. Singing? What have they got to sing about? The boys must be in school but the girls are playing some singing game, clapping and stamping. The aroma from the cooking pot is calling loudly to me. A lizard on the wall, I can see him through one of the holes in the mosquito net, cocks his head on one side and stares thoughtfully at me. I don't intend to sleep, but I do. I'm an African girl; I could be at home here.

Sirra is shaking me.

'Rise and shine. Wash your hands and face, sit on your left hand and do your best to eat with you right hand. The honour of England is at stake.' Huh?..what? Do what?

She gathers me up and, as if I weigh the same as a feather, pops me into my chair. I'm wheeled out into the compound and parked in the shade of a Mango tree. I look up into the branches but there are no mangoes about to descend on my head.

'Wrong season' laughs one of the women.

I'm handed a small bowl of water and am bright enough not to drink it. I rinse my face and hands, then pass it on to the woman who is sitting next to me. People nod; I've got something right at last. I'm part of a circle of women. We're sitting round an old oil drum, upended in the middle of the circle. A brightly tie-dyed cloth is spread over it and a large enamel bowl of rice goes on top of that. On top of the rice is the fish and on top of the fish is the sauce. There are no knives and forks. There are no spoons. Everyone is looking at me. Sirra mimes something. She's putting her fingers in her mouth. Really, manners! I'm an idiot. She's signing to me to start eating. With my fingers. Gives a new meaning to fish fingers. I use only my right hand. It doesn't help. Maybe seven grains of rice reach my lips. I've re-distributed the rest of the handful onto the top of the oil drum. I look round. Why is there no sinkhole when you really need one? I look at my fellow diners. They are all suddenly tucking into their lunch. Not a single grain of rice escapes their lips. They've done this before. One of the ladies detaches a sizeable chunk of fish from the bone and drops it onto the rice in front of me. I glance left and right. Sirra nods. I seize the fish and eat it. Delicious. Really truly tasty. I add some rice. More fish appears in front of me. I smile my thanks and devour it. Gambian food is wonderful. Within minutes the bowl is empty.

I'm feeling amazingly proud of myself. I have eaten a meal. Wow! Wait till I tell thecrowd at college. Jodie feeds herself. Headlines. Hold the front page! What does that mean, exactly? We all wash our hands again. I wash my right hand up to elbow. It's amazing, the places fish can reach.

One of the children, a pretty child, about eight years old, is holding my hand and trying to drag me along. I get the chair into action and follow her as she runs round to the back of the row of houses. She stops near another tree, not a mango this time, and grubs about in the loose soil near the roots. She pulls out a stone and some sort of toy, a little cart with wheels. Not wheels, crown corks nailed onto the wood. One of the wheels falls off and the child searches frantically for the nail which held it in place. I see it and point it out to her. She grabs it then turns to me with a smile that splits her face in two and hugs me. Now I see the point of the stone. She's using it as a hammer to nail the crown cork wheel back on. I see her through the eyes of the Neolithic girl who first used my flint scraper. I have seen invention. This little girl, the living true descendant of people of genius.

   I talked to Sirra about this little girl as we drove back the long way round to her home.

'Yes, I saw Fatou Manneh drag you off. She showed you one of her toys? You were lucky; she must have taken a liking to you. She's a bright little thing. Never been to school of course. Girls stay home to look after the babies; boys go and get an education, if they're lucky. I kept thinking about little Fatou Manneh. She seemed to be linked to me, somehow. I didn't understand it but it was to do with the tool making thing. She needed a hammer, she'd found something that would serve the purpose. Sirra was talking again. '…she's about eight years old, I think. In another five or six years she might be married, some man might take her as his third or fourth wife. Yes, polygamy's still practised here. If she was a child in Europe hopefully some teacher would have spotted her intelligence and had a chat with her mum … possibly. You would hope so, anyway. My father was determined I should get an education and, fortunately I took to it. I was lucky; I had great teachers who kept me hard at work, though it didn't seem like work till later. Tomorrow, if you like, we'll go to the Strip and you can see how other girls turn out. let's go home and settle in for the night. You can meet Binta too.'

'Binta?'

'Yes. My co-wife. I am Ed's first wife and then he married Binta. She is his second wife.'

'Oh, sorry. I didn't know you were divorced.'

'I'm not. We're both married to Ed. Binta's like a sister to me. Wait till you meet her - don't look like that! I arranged everything. Then I thought I'd made a dreadful mistake and then I knew I hadn't.' I felt like putting my fingers in my ears and going 'Rhubarb rhubarb rhubarb ….' I'd nearly gone mad when I read Max's 'Dear Jodie' letter. I could have killed him. Could I share him with Marlene? Like hell I could. Yet here was this beautiful, sensible, educated, intelligent African woman sharing her man with this Binta creature. Why? What a day this had been. What a mad mood I'm … open air toilets and shower rooms, eating fish with my fingers, seeing a child genius at work, and now listening to a cool calm older woman smilingly tell about a situation that would have any European woman screaming for her lawyer. I was imagining my Dad coming home and telling Mum he was bringing Miss Ann Other to share their bed. She'd kill him. Course she would. Wouldn't she? We were home. Sirra parked the car and lifted my chair from the back. I swung into it and headed for the house. Somebody was singing. A young woman was banging pots about in the kitchen. 'Hello, Miss Jodie. Sorry I wasn't here to greet you when you arrived the other day. I had to go shopping in Senegal. So I'm here now and I cook you shrimps Benechin. I hope you like it? Hello Sirra, my sister. How is the day?' and she bounded across the kitchen and they hugged one another. I knew my jaw had dropped open. This must be Binta, the other woman. It was. Sirra introduced us. I managed to shake her hand. She managed to hug me.

We ate the meal. It was delicious. I was worried about the amount of weight I must be putting on. It was obvious that Binta and Sirra were best mates. I couldn't see it. I would have killed Max's new girl if I could have got my hands on her. All Sirra would say was

'Binta needed help. Ed was kind enough to help her when I asked him to.' I bet he was, she's beautiful. And funny. And a great cook. What else could a man want? I just don't get it. How could Sirra tolerate it? For years? Yet here they are, laughing uproariously at some joke, arms round one another. I really don't get it. I lay awake for a long time that night, still worrying about it. The whine of a mosquito on the prowl didn't help either. I thought of that mozzy net with the huge holes in; that bothered me too. How do these people manage? They're not stupid, they cope with almost impossible situations that I've never imagined, and they laugh and smile and love. So many of the folk at home moan and whinge endlessly about quite unimportant things, not matters of life and death like people here face daily.

Eventually I drifted off to sleep. Sirra woke me far too early. I had a shower in the wet room, breakfast out on the veranda and then we were off in the car to meet people. The Strip is the main tourist area, full of hotels and banks and souvenir shops and cafes. And beggars. Beggars on wheel chairs: not so much chairs as flat pieces of board with casters on. I was reminded of man-sized versions of Fatou Manneh's little toy truck. Girls without legs, a young man with neither arms nor legs, a blind man, a stream of handicapped people begging for a few dalasi's, for a piece of fruit, for a taxi fare home, people trying to sell you cream to make your skin white or your hair straight or make you partner sex mad for you.

'Give me your wheels, you are rich, you can pay a man to carry you! Give me your shoes, you do not need them, give me money to bury my wife, my mother, my child. Please, give me bread, please, I need a sheep to celebrate my marriage, money, give me money or my children will starve, pay me and I will sleep with you;'

'You see how it is' said Sirra. 'You do not have such problems in England?'

'We do, but not so much. There are homeless people and beggars, but they don't bother you so much. The police would not allow it.' But what did I know? Maybe there were desperate people in the big cities?

'Look' said Sirra. 'See that man, the one with a wheelchair almost like yours? He works for a living. He visits the hotels and guests employ him to bring them cigarettes or bottles of water, small things like that. He has a good chair which is reliable and he can travel to the shops and return with the goods to the client in the hotels. He is honest and does not run away with the money. He gives the correct change and the clients tip him well. He is respected. But he needed a good chair to help him work. The other men and women, those with bits of board with small caster wheels, they cannot do these things so they must sit and beg.' I was beginning to get an idea. It was not my idea. Sirra had planted a thought and left it to grow in my head. Hospitals had lots of wheelchairs, some a little bit damaged like ones I had mistreated in the past, ones that would need a little repair. What happened to those, I wondered. There must be stacks of crutches too, that were perhaps not worth the cost of repairing? What else might be rattling round the rubbish tips, worthless in England but life-changing here? Sirra was smiling at me.

'Come on, I'll buy you an ice-cream.' She led me into the poshest hotel. The guard on the gate practically bowed double when he saw her; 'Good morning, Madam Sirra. How is the day? How are the family? Your husband, I hear he is working up-country? The family, are they all there? How is Madam Binta? She cooks today? Please greet her.' This elaborate greeting was repeated several times as we progressed towards the swimming pool. Not that I understood a word of it, of course, but Sirra translated it for me as we licked chocolate chip ices in the shade of yet another Mango tree.

'Tomorrow we will go to school. It is the school I attended, the school where I first taught before I became a head teacher, and it is the school where my son, Lamin, is now the head. It is, I think, the finest school in the country and we are very proud of it. You will like it, I think.' I'd better like it, I thought, and licked the last of my ice before it melted away or fell prey to the waiting ants. The pool looked tempting. I supposed they didn't approve of skinny dipping. That reminded me of Max and a night of nice naughty events. Sirra detected my mood change.

'Wait here a moment, please, Jodie.' I waited. A long moment, then she reappeared, waving a black costume. 'There's a changing room by the pool shower, see it? Just over there?' I saw it. I checked the costume size. My size. I powered over to the changing room, stripped, embarrassed a young white woman who was try, vainly, to get changed modestly, wiggled my way into the costume, adjusted my boobs and rolled for the poolside. I heard the door of the changing room slam shut behind me. You're never going to be best mates with some people. I crawled out of the chair and into the water. Not elegantly; I'm never going to be elegant, but I was in the water, flapping my arms like wings and making progress. I saw Sirra smile and put her finger to her lips. I stopped squealing for joy and progressed, well not silently, I'd never swim silently, but a bit more quietly. I still resembled a tidal wave but there wasn't much I could do about that. Sirra was taking photographs. How did she learn to do that? Honestly, it amazes me the ease with which old people take to modern technology. You'd think they invented it. The white girl from the changing room approached the pool and tested the water with one toe. What did she expect, crocodiles? Girl eating fish? Solid water? Any way, it obviously to her liking so she slumped off to the far side of the pool and drooped herself onto a sun lounger, She stripped off her wrap and lay back, topless. Honestly, I was shocked. Where did she think she was? These tourists who came to my country and displayed themselves like meat on a slab … look, there are two boys staring at her. Has she no shame? Tourist, hey, tourist, get your bra back on! I was so disgusted that I swam full speed into the end of the pool and had to make a swift turn to make it look intentional. Sirra was trying not to laugh. And failing. I clambered out of the pool and accidentally splashed water on the girl as I wheeled past her.' 'Jodie Sonko, I'm almost ashamed of you! What will that poor young woman think?'

'What was she thinking of, flaunting her tits at those boys? I nearly died of shame!'
'No, Jodie, you nearly died of a fractured skull when you head-butted the end of the pool. Maybe it's the only way she knows of getting the boys to look at her? Perhaps she was jealous of the attention you were getting?'
'Me, Sirra, me? I was just swimming quietly along.'
'Oh, Jodie. The boys were watching your every movement. They watched you going into the changing room and they applauded when you came out. The cheered when you got into the water and when you started to swim. They were happy when they saw you were enjoying yourself. All that poor girl could think of to attract their attention was to show off her breasts. Breasts are very common among girls in the Gambia. We feed our babies with them. They would have little attraction for the boys, apart from their unusual colour. Look, the boys are coming to chat with you. They like what they see, they see your courage. Stay here and I'll find a waiter and order some drinks. Why don't you call the girl over to join us? The boys will see that you are generous and not afraid of competition.' She walked off, smiling. Was she trying to get me laid? The boys arrived, very shy now. I asked one to call the girl to join us and explained that Sirra had gone to find some drinks. Two boys and two girls sat in silence round the table. Our responsible adult had deserted us. I could see that she had found somebody to talk to, and was sitting at her table. She waved to me. I was not going to wave back. People might think I had set this up myself. It was Sirra's fault; let her take the blame. The girl spoke.
'Where are you from, which village?'
'I'm from Appleton.'
'Where's that?'
'Sort of half way between Liverpool and Manchester.'
'But that's in England.'
'Of course it is. I'm English.'

'You can't be, you're black, you're a ni…' She fell silent, but her mouth was still open. The boys stood up and walked away. One of them stopped, turned back and looked at me.

'I'm sorry, Miss. We cannot stay where such language is used. I apologise. Welcome to our country. This other person might be more welcome in her own land.' Sirra was watching. I put my brain cell into gear.

'Gentlemen, please come back. I would like to chat with you. I'm sure my friend meant no harm, she spoke without thinking. We all make mistakes. I glared at her and she had the grace to look ashamed. Sirra had left her friend and was walking back to our table. The boys sat down, then seeing Sirra, sprang to their feet again. Sirra waved them down, smiled at the girl and asked her name.'

'I'm Andrea, Andrea Campion. I'm staying at the Baobab Tree Hotel with my mum and dad.' The boys were all attention. They were gazing at her legs. Naked legs. Wow. It occurred to me that I'd seen a fair number of boobs during my stay, especially in the village compound yesterday. Babies needed food. Even I knew that. But I hadn't seen any bare legs. Plenty of long skirts, trousers, wraps in beautiful patterns but no bare legs. Well, well. And here were two long, bare, white legs inviting inspection. What could be going on in the minds of the two young men? Live and learn, girl. I think she got the message because she pulled her wrap tightly round her and looked for an escape route. The boys exchanged glances, nodded and smiled. The younger one bounced to his feet - how I hate people who can do that - and offered to escort Andrea back to her hotel. Sirra agreed that if she had an escort nobody else would trouble her. The girl smiled, thanked Sirra for the drink, shook my hand and said how brave I was, and left firmly holding the hand of her escort. Sirra was off again, muttering about having to talk to the manager about hiring the hotel for a conference sometime next month. And then there were two. I looked at him. He stared at the horizon. The horizon was actually a rather pretty black girl carrying a tray of drinks to our table. I automatically hated her until Boy Two greeted her as 'sister' and asked after her twins. She gave a quick account of their genius and told him his mother was expecting him to call her and not neglect her any longer. He nodded eagerly and looked chastened. He looked even more downcast when Sirra reminded him that his mother was the most important person in his life and he should honour her and do everything in his power to help and support her. I felt almost sorry for him but added my agreement with Sirra's advice. As soon as Sister had left he brightened up and started to ask me questions about my husband and how many children I had and how much my wheelchair had cost. Sirra butted in and told him that in my country it was thought rude to ask too many questions and that he should wait until I was ready to give him answers and that might be never especially if I thought he was being too cheeky or asking too many questions or … I felt quite sorry for him and asked him about his tribe and family. We chatted for a while then he asked if I wanted to swim again. Sirra shook her head and I made the excuse that we had to go home soon. He tried to make a date for tomorrow but I put him off. I had a not quite right feeling about him and, in the car going home, Sirra agreed with me.

'There are many poor people in the Gambia. It is the duty of the eldest son to support the family if the father is no longer able to care for them. If the family is poor even the boys may not have been educated so finding employment is difficult. The boys try to make a living any way they can. They are not criminals but you must realise, Jodie, that people like you are seen as millionaires by these boys. They are mainly boys, but some of the girls, the young women, are exploited by many male tourists, evil men who prey on them for sex. They make promises which they have no intention of keeping, and abuse them. It is against the law but often by the time the crime is investigated the men are thousands of miles away. So the boys exploit the tourist women. They offer excitement, promise marriage, and demand expensive presents. Did you see the watch the boy who went off with Andrea was wearing? If it is real it would cost hundreds of pounds. Some foolish, lonely woman may indeed have given him a present in return for sex with such a young man. It happens. People try to make a living. It is not a noble way of earning money but in the end children may be educated, elderly relatives may have hospital treatment, food is put on the table. Who am I to say it is wrong. Would your mother refuse bread earned by your prostitution? We none of us can know what length we may be forced to. God will judge us, mercifully, I believe.'

I looked round; palm trees, a monkey watching from a wall, a motionless lizard. Birdsong. Children, laughing. Not a cloud in the sky. It might have been a world away from the poverty I had seen the day before. What would it take for me to become a sex worker? Max had used me, free of charge. My foster father, the plank, had abused me, raped me. The schoolboy had raped me. No money had changed hands; did that make it better or worse? What would I have done to try to save my first mother's life? What is love? I looked across at the sun lounger where Andrea had draped herself, bait on display. Was she now, as I sat safely with Sirra, finding out the cost of her morning's display? I was silent as we drove home. I noticed Sirra glance across at me but I didn't feel like responding. What would I do in those circumstances? I don't know. I still don't know.

Could I behave like Binta and become a second wife? I'd chatted with her a couple of nights ago and it seemed clear that she loved Sirra, she loved their husband, she loved their joint children and was proud of all of them. How could that be? There was more to this world than I expected or understood. I wanted to visit a school, to mix with children and enjoy their innocence and laughter. Sirra had it all planned.

Sirra had decided to send me off to school on my own.

'You are a student? You have attended several schools during your life as a student? You intend to study at University? Then nothing you see will alarm you. Look, there, across the compound. You see the gate? You turn left out of the gate. You take the next turn right and the school is directly in front of you. You cannot miss it. It has high walls which have big pictures of animals painted on them. There are no other walls like that in the village. I know because I helped to paint them. You may also notice sixty children going through the gateway into the school. I think you will have difficulty getting lost. I was being laughed at. I nodded bravely.

'Good. That is settled then. At seven o'clock tomorrow morning you start school. All week. You will work as an intern. That means you will teach every class, tell stories, sing songs, answer questions and play games. You'll be fine. You will receive no pay. Let me see your lesson plans before you leave.'

'What? Lesson plans? Play games? Me? I'm in a wheel chair. Games?' I was on the point of asking if she was either mad or blind but I do have one functioning brain cell. I made out a lesson plan. It began with the words: INTENT: to survive the day and come safe home. Not to stand tiptoe - that would be silly.

Sirra looked at it and remarked that it was a bit ambitious but I might surprise myself. I didn't sleep well. I had been a monster at school, especially with supply teachers who didn't know where everything was. I deserved hell. The time came to be brave. I painted my nails, combed my hair and wheeled out across the already hot sand to school.

Mr Ed-Lamin Edwards greeted me. Son of Sirra and Edward Edwards the bigamist. Husband of Sirra and Binta. That was just the father, what would the son be like? Son was charming.

'Good morning, Miss Sonko. I know my mother's tricks so I got here early to greet you. You like the animals on the walls? My mother's idea. Beware, I respect and love my mother but she has inherited my father's sense of humour. Nobody is safe. Come and drink Atayah then I'll show you round. Don't run over that lizard!'

It was going to be alright. A steady trickle of children came into to greet us. I lost count of all the Lamins and Fatous who curtsied and greeted me. 'Good morning, teacher, good morning Miss Sonko. My name is whatever. I hope you are well?' All in English. All in English, perfectly spoken by children. Four and five year olds. I crossed my fingers. Maybe the day would be fine.

'Miss Sonko, why do you cross your fingers? Is it to keep the devil away?' God, these kids are perceptive!

'Sorry, Fatou. It is just a habit I have.

'Miss, is it a good habit or a bad habit?'

'I'm not sure, Lamin. What do you think?' Head teacher Ed-Lamin smiles at me.

'Miss Sonko, I think you will be a good teacher. You answer a question with a question and that encourages the child to think for himself!' Maybe I will survive the day. I learn that Mr Mo-Lamin has encouraged his pupils to question teachers, so long as they do it politely. There is great respect in Gambia for elders and it isn't usually encouraged but here in this school it is OK.

The day goes well. I tell each of the four classes a story and sing them a nursery rhyme. The children tell me a story and then sing the song back to me. I'm amazed by how well they listen and remember exactly what I say. We end the day by playing a whole school football match. I, in my wheelchair, am on the United team and Mo-

Lamin with half the staff, is on the City team. My team wins by four hundred goals to 375. A fair result. After school we teachers sit on the veranda and drink green tea and chat about the world. Ed-Lamin was a student in England during the Troubles, just before I was born. He was enslaved and tortured. I hear things that have been deliberately written out of English history but which happened just before I was born. He speaks without bitterness, but described a very horrible time. He had loved an English girl and they had planned to marry but that was made impossible. His girlfriend was punished by being forced into prostitution. They escaped and made it back to the Gambia but she was weakened by her suffering and died soon after arrival. An English girl, another escapee, took care of him, saved his life, and they married and still lived together. He promised we would meet later in the week. He walked back to his parent's compound with me. He was charming, funny and very bright. Why was I so attracted to men like him? I'd have taken him to bed in a flash but I knew he wasn't for me. His adventures tied him to his wife. They had shared so much, and survived so well, it would have been an evil act to come between them. It was odd, this supposed holiday, this trip to find my roots. I wasn't learning about my ancestors, I was learning about me. I was being made to think about how I might react under duress. I was looking at the world through new eyes. My broken body was learning that it wasn't broken; it was still mine to dispose of how I wanted. I often found myself thinking that I wasn't defined by my disabilities; I was still me, Jodie Sonko. And now I was finding out just who Jodie Sonko was.

We trundled back into Sirra and Binta's compound. I learned to look on them as equals though different. Binta was certainly the better cook. Sirra could dish up a meal that would feed you but Binta's cooking of a similar menu had flavour and subtleties either missing or hidden in Sirra's meals. I noticed but didn't comment. See - I told you I'd changed!

I was welcomed in every compound I visited. I learned to greet everyone with the same words and the same dignity. If a four year old child spoke to me I listened. I learned not to question older people who did not know me very well: I listened and learned. Because I was accepted, and I was accepted because Sirra accepted me, I was expected to earn my keep. An empty lap was soon occupied by an infant while the mother went off to draw water from the well or rush off to the village shop to buy herbs or onions or dried fish. I forget how many babies I nursed, sang to, gave rides on my wheelchair or simply rocked to sleep. I transported very small children from one compound to the next, drank far too many glasses of hot sweet mint tea and accepted too many invitations to join in a meal when it was apparent there was barely enough food in the pot to feed the family. Sirra advised me it would be a huge insult to refuse but, if I wished, it was quite acceptable to take just a few grains of rice or a morsel of fish, and then declare how delicious it was. Honour would be satisfied. I did this, and every time I did I was encouraged to empty the bowl. The family would have gone hungry if I did but I learned to smile and apologise for my poor appetite. Something I did find difficult to handle was the constant stream of requests for money. Sometimes it might be a joke: 'Hey, Girl on wheels! Buy me a car and I will drive you to London!'

'Hey, Jodie, my housie has fallen down; I need a thousand Dalasi for cement!' Sometimes the requests were a little threatening: 'Jodie, give me your shoes, you will never need them …' There was one young man, Solomon, who pestered me for days for money. He needed a car, a fishing boat, a gun to hunt with, a new roof for his father's house, a dress for his girlfriend (but I could wear it if I slept with him). It all became rather threatening until I had a word with Ed-Lamin one morning. He could see that something had upset me, and that I'd arrived late for school on a couple of mornings. I felt quite guilty because I hadn't been able to deal with the pest myself. Ed-Lamin was very quietly angry. He walked off quite rapidly and I learned later he had a word with the Alkalo, who passed it on by the boy's grandfather to his mother, and had worked wonders. The boy was deeply ashamed that the whole village knew of his disgrace that he left to find work on the tourist strip, something his family had been encouraging him to do for months. I felt really sorry for him. He was a pain, but behind it all I think he'd been trying to help his family.

'Jodie.'

'Sirra? What's up?' She was looking serious.

'Jodie, I need your help. You are free to refuse. I have a proposal and I want you to consider it seriously. Do not think you have to say "yes" or "no" before you have given it a lot of thought.' What? She wants to marry me? Proposal? What's that all about?

'Jodie, you know I teach at the University? I would like you to help me.'

'Yes, right, I can make tea, coffee, hand the biscuits round? Sure, could be fun. When?'

'When is easy, anytime you like. You got the job wrong. I teach a class of very talented young women, about your age, maybe a little older. They rarely, if ever, have the chance to meet somebody like you. Some of them have met European men and do not have a good opinion of them. Oddly, not all African women are raging sex machines. That's what they think of Westerners. Maybe they're right. I have been lucky with the man in my life. But you are a woman, similar age, half Mandinka, educated and intelligent. I want them to see similarities, not differences. I would like you to take part in a free range discussion: ask questions, answer questions. Questions about anything you might be interested in, same for them. Two hours? More or less. Ideally you will learn and they will learn. I am too old; I'm an elder, a lecturer, a professor. They find it unnatural to question me, disrespectful. You are their equal, from another culture. They only know that you are an athlete and a friend of mine.'

'Wow. I can't. I've never done anything like this. I can't. How many of them?'

'Probably about a dozen at the most, first time.'

'First time? Are you …'

'Jodie, you have faced difficulties all your life. You are brilliant at coping, at making success out of disaster. Honestly. Don't you know just how much people respect you?' I didn't bother to answer that. Poor Sirra. I'd heard it happened to old people, this loss of reality. She was off again.

'So, we get there first thing in the morning, after breakfast. I booked a small room in the Drama department. It'll be quite private. Don't worry if you run over time, you've got the room all day if you want it. You can have lunch with them and swap ideas. That's what it's all about. OK? Jodie, how's it sound to you?' She expected a polite answer? It sounded like the most stupidest idea on the planet. Maybe the Dinosaurs had tried a similar approach to a discussion with Spacemen with laser guns. I just looked at her.

'OK, then? We'll start early, get there in time for a coffee, then Security can smuggle you into the theatre? I'll introduce you then get out of your way. Thank you so much. I'll buy you an ice-cream on the way home.'

'Theatre? You said theatre?'

'Yes, Lecture Theatre 7. You'll love it, nice and comfy.' I decided to go into silent mode. Silence was golden. I backed out of the room and headed for the shower.

Maybe I could wash the whole horrible idea away. A hot shower solves all worries, that's what I say. Pity that the water was freezing cold. Bugger.

Next day was sunny. All days were sunny. Why not? What had the Sun got to worry about? Sun wasn't going to confront a dozen Amazon warriors, armed to the teeth with brains, looking for the blood of the invader. Do they have Air/Sea/College Rescue on speed dial here? I don't remember breakfast. It would have been sweet Sorrel tea with fried onion baguettes but I don't remember. I don't remember the drive to the College. It took forty-five minutes but I don't remember it. I thought the policeman who was checking the traffic would save me, but he just chatted to Sirra about how well his eldest daughter was doing, working in the bank. I don't remember the herd of goats skittering about the road opposite to the SOS Children's Home. Sirra parked in the space marked Reserved: Professorial Staff Only. I don't remember being escorted to the Lecture Room, with the little glass panel in the door. A group of terrifying young women were sitting in a semi-circle of cosy looking chairs. Facing them was a small table with a jug and glass.

'Wait here, I'll call you in when I've had a word with the students. Just wait. They'll love you.' They'll love me spit roasted and smothered in Benechin sauce. I'm toast. The huge Security Guard was chatting.

'See, that small girl, the one with the black headscarf? She's my niece. A very clever girl. She's very excited about meeting you.' They were all wearing black headscarves. They all looked similarly intimidating. Sirra had finished her talk. The girls rose to their feet, clapping and smiling. The guard threw the door open and I rolled in to face the storm. The girls stopped applauding and curtsied. As one they said

'Good morning, Miss Sonko. How are you today? We are very happy to meet you.' I looked round but Sirra had escaped. The girls were still standing. I recalled the infant school classes.

'Good morning, ladies. I am very happy to meet you. Please sit down.' I rolled into the room and took up station alongside the table. If I threw the jug at the most active enemy I might make my escape. No, it wouldn't work. One of the girls was speaking.

'Miss Sonko, how is it possible that you are an athlete? You cannot even walk, I think? My name is Fatou.' Start at the deep end, why don't you?

'Fatou, thank you for your question. Before I had my accident I loved running. It was my escape from school.'

'You wanted to escape, escape from school? How can that be? If you are fortunate and have a place in school why would you run away?'

'I would run away because I am black, Fatou. All the other children were white. They called me names and pulled my hair and made fun of me. I hated it so I ran away.'

'But that is not lawful. The police and the teachers would arrest the culprits.'

'I do not agree. True, the teachers would say it was a bad thing to do but they went on doing it. I did not think of calling the police because they, because I do not know why I did not call them. I did not tell my mother because it would upset her. She died when I was still young and I was put into a care home and then given to foster parents. That was bad, because the man assaulted me. Then there was a car crash and they were killed and I broke my back. So now I run on wheels. It is my sport.'

There was a pause while the girls digested the suggestion that it might for some reason, be bad to be black in a white country. One of them wanted to try the chair. I asked a couple of strong looking young women to help me onto one of the easy chairs, then each of the girls did a circuit of the room, very carefully, on my wheels. They managed without too many collisions with the furniture and returned to their seats looking thoughtful.

'Miss Jodie, this is a very special chair?' 'Yes, it's for travelling. It's light and it folds up to fit in the back of a taxi. At home I have a racing chair which is even lighter, with only three wheels. It is very fast and I use it for racing.'

'Racing? Really? There are other people who race chairs?' I explained about the Paralympics. They changed the topic.

'Miss, you have a boyfriend?'

'Yes.'

'Is he, a …, is he a cripple too?'

'We don't like to use that word. My first boyfriend was not handicapped. Sadly, he found he did not like me because I am. My boyfriend now, he is like me. We started to race one another at school. Now we ..'

'Now you don't need to race?'

'No. Well, sometimes we race. It's a game.'

'Now you can play other games, miss?'

'Yes, we play rugby and basketball, and we …'

'Miss, do you play games like we do with our boys?' She was laughing. So was the whole class, giggling and self-conscious. Ah, those games!

'Yes, Fatou, we play those games too.'

'Miss, have you been cut?'

The giggling stopped. I had the feeling that a boundary had somehow been crossed. Silence. I must have looked blank.

'Miss, do girls in England, young girls, get sent to be cut when they're about five years old?'

'Sorry, I'm not with you, I don't understand?' Silence, then

'Miss, cut like, like circumcised?' Silent scrutiny of my face.

'Girls, circumcised? How? Some boys are circumcised, I think. But how can a girl be?' Glances were exchanged, heads shaken. Somewhere outside a bell rang. Nobody moved.

'Miss, I'm sorry. My question disturbs you, I think?' The very bright niece of the security man, I think. Small, black headscarf. What's with the headscarves?

'Yes, I'm sorry. I don't understand your question. I just don't know. I think the answer is no, girls aren't cut, but, honestly, I don't know how it could be done to girls?'

'Miss, the place where your husband makes love to you, you know, that place is sewn up and only a small pee hole is left. The lips are cut away, that's what is sewn up. Then your husband knows you are a true virgin. The pain of the circumcision is to make you brave and prepare you for the pain of your husband opening you and for the pain of childbirth. That is what it is for. It is our culture. Miss, I have disturbed you. Sorry.'

The other young women were nodding. A small round of applause.

'She explains it well. I was cut at the same ceremony; she was the bravest of all of us.'

'And she is brave to explain it to Miss Sonko.' I nodded. I could not have spoken to any of my teachers about such things, not even Miss Ellesmere. I asked how many of the girls had been cut. Slowly ten hands went up. One of the girls who was not cut spoke;

'Miss, we are sisters; our father would not permit the operation. He said it was dangerous and unnecessary, but we are not sure he was right. Not having been cut may make it difficult to find a husband. Maybe boys will think we are prostitutes?'

Time to change the subject, perhaps. I'd ask Sirra if she had expected this line of discussion. Let's try something a little milder.

'Right, ladies. I need time to think about this, I am learning more from you than you are from me, I'm afraid.'

'No, miss. We are learning what you do not know and that is a valuable lesson for a student. Please, can we question you about other matters?'

Questions about other matters sounded good.

'O.K. I'd like that.'

'Miss, would your father kill you if you had a lover and he found out?'

'Miss, do you have a lover?'

'Miss, has your father found you a husband and if so, must you marry him?'

'Miss, can a woman divorce a man in your country?'

'Miss, is it possible to ...'

'Stop! I will try to answer your questions: my father has not murdered me because I had a lover. That boy turned out to be a bad man who abused me. I was foolish and I will not see the man again. I don't have a boyfriend at the moment but I do have a good friend who is a boy, a young man. My father will not kill him, neither will I be forced to marry him.'

'Miss, what is his name?'

'My father's name is William Wills, but I call him Dad. Most people call him Bill. I'm not telling the name of my boyfriend; it's not official, we're not engaged or anything ...'

35

Ed-Lamin had taught me how to use Skype so we could keep in touch. I kept forgetting that he was as English as I am and that he'd been to Uni here. I'd never thought of myself as racist, but being surprised that a middle-aged African could be miles ahead of me as far as technology was concerned was a lesson I deserved to learn.

By the time my supposed holiday ended I was exhausted, happy, had met wonderful people, loved the life they led and couldn't wait to get back. I cried all the way to the airport, I cried all the time I was in the waiting area, cried my way onto the plane and for most of the six-hour flight I continued to cry. I cried because I'd left Sirra and Ed and Binta and Ed-Lamin and all the rest of the family. I cried because I'd left sixty little school children, all real characters, and their teachers. I was missing all the people I'd chattered to, greeted and laughed with. And I cried for the times when I wasn't treated like some bloody curiosity or freak show. I was treated as an equal. I was a sort of second rate equal because I hadn't learned much of any of the six local languages, but I gained respect for my skills, previously undiscovered, as a teacher and baby sitter and because I could laugh at myself and my mistakes, like when I drank the bowl of water that was being passed round the table so people could rinse their fingers … I did learn to watch and learn.

I arrived home with horrible belly pains. Something I'd eaten. Something I'd eaten on the plane, apparently. Half the passengers, the half who like me had the chicken, were less than happy bunnies by the time the plane landed. Serves the bunnies right for eating meat, I thought, between vomiting all over my last clean clothing. I'd left most of my belongings with Binta, who had promised to find good homes for them. It certainly helped my dash out of the airport. None of the armed guards seemed to see me as a rogue girl assassin; they just stood aside and let me through. From the plane to the outside world and getting into Belinda? Twenty three minutes. Record. The people I felt really sorry for were the passengers who hadn't tried the chicken. I bet they got the full fall-out effects before they reached home. Bill wheeled me into my wet-room shower, closed the door and told me to emerge when I'd showered ten times, then thrown everything I'd worn in the bin, then shower again, dry, and put my robe on. Only then I could emerge and join them round the fire. Fire? Yep. Never a couple to leave a thought unfulfilled they had opened up a Medieval Hearth in the middle of the living room. Bill promised that it had every desirable safety control possible including its own telephone line to the Fire Fighters, but I could see that Sue wasn't totally convinced. God, it was good to be home again. I had a little weep about that, and then I'm told I talked non-stop for four hours about my adventures. I only stopped then because I noticed that the big plate full of homemade scones had only two left. I did, honestly I did, consider taking both round to the old lady who lived all by herself next door. Then I remembered that the old lady I was thinking of lived three thousand miles away and I would have eaten both scones and crumbs and probably the plate as well by the time I got there. I should, as a good Gambian girl, have offered both scones to my respected elderly parents, but because fifty per cent of me wasn't Gambian, and because the respected elders had scoffed all the other scones, I just grabbed and ate. It was good to be home, but my other home was calling quite loudly to me.

My excuse for sleeping for the next twenty hours was that I'd managed so little sleep during my holiday and talking to the elders had been a strain and besides, I'd forgotten just how comfortable my own bed was. I loved the circular hearth and eventually hauled myself out of bed and invaded the realm of Elder. They had only bloody gone out and left me, home alone. Never before, in all my eighteen years on this planet had I been left alone. God only knows what might have happened. True, the anti-burglar devices took Bill twenty minutes to fully disarm and he'd installed the things in the first place. Serve him right if I set them off and he rushed home to find his beautiful daughter had been taken into protective custard by Cheshire's finest. I'd report myself abandoned as soon as I'd made a pot of coffee. There were still some scones left and I found a note addressed to me in the fridge, rubber banded to the milk jug:

> *Gone to collect parcel from Post Office. Back soon, Dad.*
> *Gone to buy food because you've eaten all we had to live on this year.*
> *Mum xx*

I must have bored the knickers off most of my year group. As I was rambling on, hour after hour, about tribal customs and costumes I could see them pairing up, creeping away, hand in hand, glancing back to see if I'd noticed their desertion. FGM emptied the room almost completely, only Hank was left. I'd intertwined my wheels with his and he'd have to put some considerable effort into disentangling us. Oddly, he showed no hint of wishing to do so. Eventually I shut up and offered to buy him a drink. So we rolled off to the student bar. It took quite a long time because for one thing, the bar was at the far end of a long corridor and for another different but closely related thing, it seemed like a good idea for Hank to power my offside wheel with his right hand and for me to power his near side wheel with my left hand and that every time we collided we should mutually apologise with a kiss. It was a really stupid idea because it was nearly closing time when we reached the bar. Nearly, but not quite. He bought me a bitter shandy and he attacked a pint of Fosters. I helped him to drink his and found it quite to my liking. I explained to him the tea ritual, the availability of orange drinks, the taste of Julbrew, the local larger, and the importance of Malta, non-alcoholic but guaranteed to make the drinker strong. I explained the nature of 'strong' in this context. He blushed. We ended up sharing the back seat of a taxi to his house. I'd already met his mum and dad at some to the sporting events and they didn't seem too amazed to see me wheeling alongside their son. The house had been adapted for boys on wheels and Hank's bedroom was where the front room would be in most other houses. I noticed that it had a good-sized bed, an en-suite loo and shelves of books and a desk with jumbled papers and a laptop. His mum brought in a tray with mugs of something and a plate of chocolate biscuits, smiled at her son, said 'About time too.' She placed the tray on a clear bit of the desk and was about to leave when SBB opened her stupid mouth and asked
'Shall I be mum?' Hank's mother said nothing, but she gave her son a long, steady, killer mum look that said quite plainly what we were all thinking. She walked out of the room, closing the door quietly behind her.
What happened next? Two randy eighteen year olds, together in a room with a very comfortable double bed? Plus a tray of hot chocolate and chocolate biscuits? What do you think happened?

37

I met mum in town the next morning for coffee and cakes in Golden Square. It's odd; isn't it, how you accept odd place names because they're in the town where you grew up? Golden Square isn't Golden. And how about Slutcher's Lane? Who was Slutch? Bridge Street and Hill Top are fairly obvious. Wilderspool Causeway? How about that for an address? It's where my flat is, but who or what was Wilderspool? Some gent out of a Dickens novel? See, I'm reading. And I'm rambling and rabbiting. Are they the same thing? And you know why I'm rabbiting or rambling. In about five minutes I'm going to be facing mum across a small coffee shop table the morning after the night before. Not that we'd done anything illegal or abnormal. We're both old enough to vote or join the army or get, or get … no, ignore that one. I'm old enough to get pregnant, but I'm not. Can't be. I am old enough to visit the chemist and get a morning after pill, not that I need to. Hank was very careful. We both were. God, I must keep a straight face. Sue can read me like a Kindle. Stop grinning, Jodie. Where's Rachel when I need her? Only there is a real Rachel now. Ed-Lamin's wife is called Rachel. Rachel Shaw. She's fantastic. She used to bunk off school because she was an outsider too. Only she didn't go running, she went sailing. And her sailing saved her life, and Ed-Lamin's life, and the lives of her mum and dad, and it would have saved the life of Jane, Ed-Lamin's fiancée, only she got malaria after they'd all landed safely in West Africa, where Rachel had sailed them to protect them from the English Troubles. She and Binta run a sort of boat-building school so village women can build small fishing boats - you must have seen her on the TV News at times?
'Have a good time last night?' It's that girl from the other coffee shop, the girl with just the one hand.
'Hi! Hello, how are you doing? What last night?'
'So, that last night with Hank? He's raving about you! He's a sort of cousin by adoption, don't worry, he's a really good guy. Time he had a girl to keep him in order. Hello, Mrs Wills, how are you?' Trust Mum to arrive at the world's most embarrassing moment.
Why is there never a sinkhole when you want one? Sinkholes eat people's cars and houses and railways but can you ever rely on there being a very deep, one metre square one when you need to drop out of society for a while, twenty years or so?
 'Hello, love. How's the course going?'
'Good, thanks. I'm doing the units on running your own business, taxation, employment law, that sort of stuff. Black coffees and croissants? Fresh cooked this morning?' She smiled and left us to it. Daughter no longer a pure innocent maid, even if she wasn't before. This wasn't rape. Well, not by him. He hadn't had much choice, once the hot chocolate was drained.
'Morning, Jodie.'
She's going to ask if the sexy undies came in handy. I just know she is.
'Morning mum. Where's dad?'
'He's having fun parking Belinda. He'll be along any hour now.'
'Mum …'
'Daughter, if it's going to be one of those too much information days can you wait till your dad gets here?'
'What?'
'Saved by the coffee bean. Drink up and think what you really want to tell me. '
'Mum, I'm happy.'

'Good. That's good, Jodie. We love you, you know. Your Dad's got something to tell you, if he ever gets here. I could tell you but that would spoil it for him. You might be pleased, too. Sirra rang last night and … oh, good, here he is. Go and get him a coffee will you, love?'

I have my uses. I trundled off back to the counter. It's good, being asked to do things. Makes you part of the family, even if it is a pain sometimes. Coffee, croissant and a bit more info about Hank. Knocked down by a hit and run driver when he was a toddler, Duke of Edinburgh Gold Award, saved somebody's life by doing mouth to mouth, all sorts of things. And he'd never thought of mentioning it. I'd have been shouting about it all, all the time. Wait till I see him again. Four hours and seventeen minutes. That's weeks away. I'll be old and grey and careworn and … and he's here! The only coffee shop in town with room for two racing chairs and he has to roll into this one. I can't even wave unless I sacrifice Dad's coffee. Ah, he's seen me. He's smiling. I don't even know what sort of coffee he drinks. Maybe, if brain cell engages, I could ask him?

'Hi, Jodie, Americano, if you're buying?'

Five minutes later, two couples at one table. I'm a couple. I'm grinning like a very grinning thing. I must stop staring at Hank. Only if he stops staring at me. I try to drink my coffee and miss my mouth. I try the croissant and choke on the crumbs. I will give up eating. And drinking. It's a very inefficient way of gaining nourishment and hydration. I've missed what Dad's saying. He's looking at me like I'm intellectually challenged. Well, I am. There's alien hormones in the air. Not my fault.

'Planet Earth to Jodie Sonko?' Who? Oh, me.

'Planet Sonko to Daddy Earth?' That came out wrong. Or did it. Just wheel me away. 'Sorry, Dad. Go on, please?'

'Put the girl out of her misery, Bill. The call was meant for her anyway.'

'Yes. It was. Jodie; Sirra would like you to go back to Malinding village with a team of people like yourself and a container full of wheelchairs, and set up a distribution and information centre in the village. A six-month visit, expenses paid by Sirra's organisation. There's an empty building, it's the old clinic, just across the road from her school. She said you'd know where she meant. We could go with you, if needed, or you pick your own team. She's sent you a file with more information. There's a small salary involved. Your university is willing to suspend your course, and for any other student you may wish to involve. The offer's open for a month.' So is my mouth. I close it and look at Hank. Looking just doesn't do. I reach across and kiss him full on the mouth. I hear crockery crashing to the floor. I don't care. I'm a couple. I am. Or am I? I climb out of Hank's mouth and look at him. He's grinning. He's saying something … it's 'Yes!' I join in. Two disabled idiots are chanting 'Yes Yes Yes Yes!'

I seem to recall a similar chant not too long ago then remember and go silent. And nobody seemed very disabled last night. We can do this. We can really do it. Thank, you Sirra. Thank you.

'My dad's firm has containers.' Hank's first contribution. He was in! I didn't have to bully him, coax him (though that might be fun); he was in, with a suggestion of practical help.

'Sounds good' said Bill. 'I'll plant a few thoughts in people's minds.' He started to work sending messages from his phone. I was so pleased I'd shown him how to do that.

I rolled across to the counter and ordered a round of coffee and cakes.

'What are your crowd up to? They sound excited?'

'I think we're starting a sort of charity thing, I'm not sure.'

'Oh. What sort of thing?'

'Providing proper wheelchairs for people who really need them. In Africa. It's for people like Hank and me to run.'

'I'm a people like that.'

I looked at her. Is that how she saw herself? I bet most folk who came into the café never noticed that she had only one hand. What was she saying? Did she see herself as being like Hank and me? Surely not. She had bags of personality, was engaged to be married, had a future planned. I looked at her. She was beautiful, and she was waiting for my reply.

'Yes' I said. 'People like you, people like you who manage so well that lots of people don't even notice that you're people like me and Hank. When can you spare a few minutes to come and chat to us?'

'Now' she said. 'I've just resigned. Somebody objected to me being employed to work with the customers. I'm unsightly it seems. I put people off their coffee. She didn't want to have anything I'd touched handed to her. Disfigured people should, she said, be kept in special hospitals and not allowed to mix with normal people.'

I was speechless. I was conditioned to be assaulted by oafs swearing at me. I was accustomed to having belongings snatched from my hands, to having my chair damaged. That's normal, I'm different. Nobody looking at me is going to mistake me for a blue-eyed blonde princess. But Sirra has seen something; I can't imagine what, that leads her to trust me with a brand new enterprise. Bill and Sue have trusted me to join their family. Hank has trusted me, I'm not sure why, to be his partner, for the moment at least. Now this young woman, despite being so horribly insulted, wants at least to get to know us better.

'Tell you what,' she said. 'I'll be your cook, your catering officer. What do you think?'

'I think that's a bloody good idea.' She walked out from behind the counter and came to sit at our table.

'Hello, I'm Alison. I'm a cook. Maybe I could be useful?' Oddly, for no reason, I was feeling tearful. Hank noticed.

'Jodie, what's the matter, love?' Love, he called me love. And he noticed I was sad.

'Just being stupid. Just wishing that my first mum could see me, and share today.' He held my hand.

'Nothing stupid about that. Normal, I'd say. Perfectly normal.'

We ended the meeting soon afterwards. Email addresses were exchanged, Sue offered Alison a lift home, Hank and I decided not to race back to his house. That lasted for all of forty-five seconds. Honestly, how to get wheelchair users a bad name! I thought about that as I relaxed on his bed later. Competiveness seemed to be a feature of our friendship. No, wrong word. Relationship. I wondered why. I was just naturally faster than he was. It didn't seem to spoil things though. He just kept trying harder. I rolled over to get a better view of him. He was smiling at me. Bugger. That's the killer. Not many people smile at me. I don't often smile at myself. But I'm beginning to. I smiled back, and that was the right thing to do.

38

I asked Bill and Sue to take over the paper work. It was their sort of thing. They insisted I read every word and agreed every action. I was the boss, they said. That was Sirra's decision and Sirra was the boss of bosses. So, I tried. Somehow, either because mum and dad were devious and manipulative or, more unlikely, because I was beginning to understand how these things work, the charity grew. Jodie's Wheels. I thought it was a daft name. I hated seeing it on every sheet of paper, followed by a long number which proved it was, is, a proper registered charity. I was out voted. Democracy, they said. The will of the people, they said. Secretly, I quite liked it. I was given the job of writing a blog about the charity and Hank helped me with that. Hank's dad said he was glad that Hank had got his hands on a good girl - me! - and gave us a great deal of help. He knew all there was to know about shipping and exporting and dealing with customs and taxes. He and dad got on really well together. Hank was pleased and promised me he would keep his hands on me wherever I liked. Alison was brilliant. Her boyfriend's a journalist and wrote about us in the local paper and even got us a spot on TV. I've got a DVD of it and still play it, or, more honestly, Hank makes me watch it when I'm feeling down. Not often, these days, but it's there. just in case.

We opened a bank account for the charity and lots of people donated money and most Gift Aided it so we could claim back any tax that had been paid. Bill and Sue, Alison, Hank and I were the Trustees. Bill said that meant that if any theft or fraud happened we would be the people who would be sent to gaol. Looking back it seems to have been easy, but it wasn't. There were hours and hours of work and I felt stupid and useless. Sue would send me out to train, just to let off steam. Hanks talked to lots of people and we put adverts for the charity on our chairs and on Van. And none of us went to prison. When we'd grown a lot, and had a lot more money, we registered as a full charity with the Charity Commission and we had to submit proper accounts and write reports. Bill was brilliant.

Sirra kept in touch nearly every day. Ed-Lamin had taught her to use a video so we could see what was happening to the old clinic building. Half had been made into a sort of warehouse and the other half had been converted into accommodation for us. Six private rooms, a living area opening onto a veranda, a kitchen - Alison was in charge - and two flush toilets with their own sewage tank.

'Just fancy' said Hank, 'a sewage tank of our very own!' He could get romantic about some very strange things. Still sewage runs deep.

Hank's family had been acquiring wheelchairs and crutches. Fortunately they were storing them for us too. His dad had listened when we were planning our next trip and he'd arranged for the container to arrive in Banjul, the capital and main port, about the same time that we did, or a day or two later. Sirra and Ed, her husband, would meet us at the airport, Binta would cook our first meal and she agreed to help Alison with our catering. We sent over some money to pay for the redecorating of the converted clinic and we paid the wages of a watchman to ensure that nothing was looted. Fact of life, as Sirra said. I felt a bit shocked that somebody might even think of robbing a charity, but as Sue pointed out, theft is an international problem. A thief is a thief: he may wear rags or he may wear a smart suit and talk with a posh voice, but a thief is a thief. It's the duty of the trustees to do all they can to make sure that the help the charity gives goes to the people who genuinely need it.

Hank had moved into my flat. It was a bit cramped, but only in a nice way. I lie. It was very cramped and it was bloody wonderful. Lust or love; who cared? We travelled together to college, we travelled together home again. We fell into the same bed, and stayed there longer than was strictly necessary. Who cared? People knew where to find us. The paperwork was completed, the container was shipped our flights were booked. Sirra and Ed were on stand-by for the flight arrival, a friend of Ed-Lamin had promised to attend the docking of the container ship and arrange onward travel to Malinding.

39

Fifty five fingers were crossed and nothing went wrong. Not very wrong. The ship
was delayed by foul weather for several days and our flight was cancelled for
mechanical reasons.

'Just think' Hank consoled me, 'when you're sitting in a plane waiting to take off, that
plane has been assembled from the cheapest possible components. One or two are
bound to be a bit duff. Stands to reason.' I hit him. Playfully, of course. It all worked
out well. We arrived, we were met, we had a great meal. Alison and Binta got on well.
They would disappear for hours as Binta guided Alison round the market, taught her
to haggle, taught her the names of the ingredients she used and taught her to cook
them like a real Gambian. Alison in return taught European cooking to a group of the
older village women with a view to them finding employment in some of the tourist
hotels. A few did so, but several of the others set up their own roadside café in a
disused double decker bus, which itself became a tourist attraction.

I liked the old clinic. The rooms were compact, but no worse than my flat on the
Causeway. The money we sent out had been well used. Binta organised the laundry,
employing a couple of young women from the village and they used the income to
feed their family and saved what they could to pay for a basic computer course.

We found that we usually had a room to spare and the Alkalo often sent us casual
visitors. This was an African tradition: turn up unannounced in a village, give the
Alkalo a small present, Kola nuts or a few candles or a small bag of rice and he,
usually a he, would direct you to a compound where you would be given a space to
sleep and provided with a meal. Next morning you would pay the host a small sum of
money and move on.

In that first month we were sent a young woman, travelling on her own through
Africa. Katie was brilliant and adopted us. She's a trained nurse, a specialist in
hospital theatre management. She helped to organise the operating theatre in the new
clinic. The nurse in charge recommended her to visit the hospital in the nearby town,
just a short journey away by bush taxi. Katie loved the work and the people and
decided to stay in the country for at least a year. Sirra persuaded her to accompany me
to one of my now regular visits to the university and Katie took to this work like a
duck. We provided her with accommodation and she, in return, kept the place in good
order. She had a natural air of authority and was much respected by the villagers.
Nobody messed with Katie!

Katie also was brilliant at spotting people who needed a wheelchair but who lacked
the confidence to apply for one. She had infinite patience teaching handicapped
youngsters to use a chair safely, having decided that I was too much of a risk-taker to
be entrusted with such a responsibility.

'Jodie.'
'Hank.'
'Are you awake?'
'No. Go away. The goat needs milking. Binta needs a lift into Banjul. I need more
sleep. Go away.'
'Jodie. Do you know how long we've been here?'
'Yes. We got into bed at ten o'clock because the generator ran out of fuel and you
were too late to fetch some more and said you had a brilliant idea which involved both
of us getting into bed and …'
'Jodie: not that. Get off me. I mean here in the village?'
'Yes. Not long enough.'

'It's time to go home. England home. Uni home. Warrington home.'

'There's no need to go anywhere. This bed is home. I like the neighbours. There's a bus that's the best coffee shop in Africa. Binta and Alison are the finest cooks on the planet. Mum and dad can come and live in room four. Katie's fun. We're part of the village.'

'We've got things to do. Stop it! We've got degrees to get. It's going to be the rainy season here and we'll get malaria and die. We can come back again next year. And the year after that we can come and live here, if we want.' The discussion rumbled on through breakfast. It was already into the second half of the match, extra time, even. We declared a truce. It was too hot to argue. Sirra looked across at me.

'Why don't you visit Amadou? He's interesting to talk to. Go to the school but keep right round the outside of the fence. If you go into the school you'll be there all day. I know my son; he'll grab any passing help. When you come to the end of the school fence stop. Look straight across the blacktop road and you'll see a house. That's Amadou's place. Mind how you cross the road because the lorries from the sand mines race along there. The drivers get paid by the number of deliveries they can make. We'd hate to lose you! Give Amadou my greetings.'

I gathered my brain cells together. It took time in the heat. I pulled a headscarf on for protection from the dust and to try to fit into the local way of life. Great. Clever. Black girl, unable to speak any local language, rolling along in a wheelchair that must have cost a year's wages, disguises herself with a bit of cloth. Brilliant. At least try not to run over any local children. Or elders. I followed directions. Don't I always? I spotted the house across the road and headed for it. A blast of air horns nearly blew me back to the old clinic. Not one sand lorry, three. Two from the left and one from the right. All trying to stay on the flat black bit of the road that was barely wide enough for a bicycle. I pulled back as hard as I could and got stuck in the sand.

'Bother and deary me' I said, or words to that effect.

'Hello, Miss Sonko. How is the day? The family, are they all there? Is there peace? You should be careful when there is traffic. Do you not have traffic in Holland? Or Germany? My father sent me to greet you. He is Amadou Bojang. Please let me escort you to our compound?'

'Please, yes please. I am Jodie. What is your name? Sorry, I must learn to greet you properly. I apologise. I am English.'

'Miss Sonko, do not apologise for your land of birth. You are a guest of Sirra's so we must respect you. Let me help you. I am Lamin Bojang, the eldest son. I have four older sisters but I am the son. Please, how best do I help?'

'Lamin, pull me back out of this deep sand then we will find a place where it is safer to cross, please.' Rescued by a ten-year-old oldest son. Great. Good job I don't have a self-image. Not a good one anyway. Together we conquered the road and a herd of overladen sand lorries. Lamin's tactic was to push out into the road and pray. It worked. We crossed. He continued to push me and I continued to let him. It was too hot to argue. He backed me in through the battered corrugated tin doors of the compound and parked me under yet another Mango tree.

'Miss Sonko, here is my father, Amadou.' I was aware of the arrival of a hundred children, all yelling 'Good morning, Miss Sonko. How are you Miss Sonko, we are fine, thank you Miss Sonko.' Well, maybe not a hundred of them. Twelve, perhaps. Mostly girls. All ages from just toddling to very graceful early twenties. And a smiling man, couldn't tell his age, greying hair, beaming at me from behind the crush. I had collected at least four of the smallest on my chair and most of the others crowded round, fingering my hair, gently touching my skin, examining my nail

polish, and the boys, on hands and knees, trying to see how my chair worked.
Amadou was trying to quieten them and pull them off me but I was quite enjoying the
attention. Yes, it was too hot, yes, the children were sweaty, snotty and noisy but I
loved it. I smiled and the questions came: where from, what name, was I married, how
many babies, how old, why wasn't I white, people in England are white, why do you
look like a Mandinka girl, where is your husband/mother/father/brothers/sisters and so
on. All together. On and on. Lamin and Amadou finally quelled the crowd.
'Miss Sonko, if you can answer as many of the questions as you can remember they
will leave you in peace, at least for a while. You are a puzzle to them. You are not
white, you do not walk, you speak only English. Please, if you speak, they will listen.
You are an elder, they will respect you. Greet them and tell your story, please.'
True enough, the audience was sitting quietly in front of me. Amadou stood at the
back, still smiling. He nodded to me. Deep breath. Me, an elder? Better get this right
then.
'Good morning, Mr Bojang, Lamin, children. Is there peace?'
'There is only peace'
'I am Jodie Sonko. I am here because Sirra invited me and my friends to visit her. I do
not walk because I was in a car that crashed. I am black because my birth father was,
or is, black. I know that my mother is dead but I have never known my father. Maybe
I look like a Mandinka because maybe my father was. My mother was white and we
do not have tribes. I don't have any brothers or sisters, unless there are some here, in
Africa, that I don't know about. In England we speak only English, but it would be
useful to speak other languages, French, German, Chinese, Polish perhaps. But
mostly, we only speak English. I am not married because, I think, of my injuries. I
may never have babies, I do not know. I do not have employment because I am still
being educated. You are part of my education, and I say thank you to all of you. I
wish you all long life, good health, and happiness. Thank you.' They stood and
clapped and smiled at me.
Amadou spoke for the first time.
'Children, thank you. You have listened well. Miss Sonko, I had heard that you are a
great teacher and now I know that is true. You omitted only to greet the Imam and the
Alkalo in their absence, but you will know to do that in future. Now, please take your
time to wash and then we will eat. My oldest daughter has cooked fish, which I
believe you like?' One of the older girls, Fatou, escorted me round the back of the
house into a fenced space.
'This is our shower. If you wish I can help you to take a full shower? I can help with
your clothing? Or you can just wash your hands, perhaps?'
I settled for the hands wash. I stretched my hands out to one side and she slowly
poured water from a plastic bucket over them, then offered a scrap of worn towel to
dry myself. She smiled and chatted and at no time did I feel that I was being pitied or
patronised or being a nuisance. I needed a little help, she was happy because she
could offer it. Equals.
Fatou directed me back through the house. Just outside the back door another young
woman was boiling rice, cleaning fish and frying vegetables. Multi-tasking in action,
and she still had time to chat to me and offered to let me join in. I made an excuse and
left. I might just manage afterwards to clean one of the pans she was using, and I
could be useful carrying water from the well but I definitely didn't wish to be famous
for poisoning a whole family. Inside the house there seemed to be just two rooms. The
one at the rear, next to the kitchen, was filled by a double bed. It had an iron frame
and was covered by layers of brightly patterned cloth.

'You can rest for a while, till the food is ready, if you wish?' Not for me; I wanted to be with the action, if there was any. The bedroom opened directly into the front room. There were a couple of woven rugs on the floor and a row of rolled-up mattresses against one wall. There were three old plastic chairs, a few upturned large paint tins and a wooden box on top of which stood a stump of candle in a saucer. There was a square hole in the front wall covered by damaged mosquito netting. The walls were unpainted. A gloomy little room. The front door was a sheet of corrugated iron, hinged on one side and fastened by a garden-shed hasp on the other. Fatou helped my chair down a step off the veranda onto the sandy floor of the compound. That was the house: outdoor kitchen and shower, two small rooms, a narrow veranda. That was it. No loo in sight, water from a well at the far side of the compound, lighting by candle. Home to Mr and Mrs Bojang and their ten, possibly twelve, children. Fatou was a mind reader.

'We big girls sleep next door in my Grandmother's compound. The older boys sleep in the house of my father's brother, my uncle. His compound backs onto this one. Only the small boys and girls sleep here.' She smiled at me. 'You see, we make good arrangements. This way everybody is looked after. When I am married, after my husband brings the Kola nuts, I will stay here and he will visit me. When I am pregnant my husband must provide me with a bed and a complete kitchen. I will then move to live with him, at his parent's compound, or, if he is rich, we will rent a compound of our own.'

'This will be a forced marriage?' I was horrified at the thought.

'Forced? Of course it's not. It is arranged. Arranged marriage is good. My father and mother, who love me, will consider who will make me happy, who will provide good care for me and who will love me. If the man agrees he will bring a present of Kola nuts to show that he is interested in having me. Then he is allowed to talk to me, and, if I agree, we will see if we can make babies. If I do not like him I can refuse, or he can refuse me. If our decision is not right, after we are married we can still divorce. If I divorce him I must repay the value of the presents. It is all very civilised.'

'But you divorce, after you have children, can you marry again?'

'Of course, and if I have boy children that would be good because I can show that I can give a man sons, and that is what every man wants. Good strong sons.'

'It's not like England. We have to find our own husbands. I don't suppose I shall marry.' She looked at me, amazed.

'But you are young, you are rich, you are beautiful. You are …'

'I am a cripple. I cannot walk or run or dance. I would be a liability for any man. I am black, and that is not a desired colour in the eyes of most men. I don't know if I will find work. A man would be mad to take me to wife.'

'I know a man who would bed you and wed you.'

'No you don't. Who?'

'Your friend Hank. It is known that his eyes follow you, and that he smiles when he sees you. It is supposed that he is your husband already. We women know the signs, and you are one of us.' I felt uncomfortable. This was getting a bit too hot for me. I'd come to know myself, and I had no great expectations. Yes, I liked Hank. I liked him a lot. I'd known him at school and on that memorable school trip to London. Anyway, he's a cripple like me. How the hell would that work? We both needed carers. Bill and Sue weren't labelled my carers, they were my mum and dad, but what they did was to care for me. They'd probably be my carers until they die, and after that, after their funeral, I'd be whisked back into a care home for the rest of my life. Same for Hank.

His mum cared for him. We might romp about a bit, and it was fun. But marriage? Nonsense and out of the question. Even if …

'Wake up, Jodie. Time for lunch. You are an important guest. My sister has served your meal in a separate bowl. My father and mother will eat from the large bowl and when they have finished, us older children will eat and then the little ones. There is plenty for all.

A cloth was placed over my lap; how did they know I was a messy eater? Then a bowl of rice, with a fillet of fish and a sauce. Tomato and onion and some sort of spice. Smelled wonderful. Yes, I was hungry. They were waiting for me to start. I put my left hand well out of the way, broke off a piece of fish and lifted it to my lips.

'Jodie, be careful, there are bones! It's a river fish, Bongo, we call it. It's delicious but there are many bones.' Yep, this little fish had enough bones for a herd of camels. Fine, hair-like things. I extracted as many as possible. Tasted good, worth the effort. I showed off my rice-eating skills. I soon attracted a flock of chickens that squabbled noisily around my wheels, where rich pickings were to be had.

'See' said Amadou, 'we have a famous guest. Chickens are coming from as far away as Bakau to greet her, and they are richly rewarded for their attention.' Not so long ago I would have thrown the bowl at him and driven over his feet in a rage. But. But now I was laughing as much as the rest of them. Besides, it was a lovely meal. I'd have been mad to throw it away. Anyway, I'd already eaten most of it. And, remember, I've been civilised. Those boys in Germany had seen to that. And Max. Max. Bugger Max, I'd learned my lesson there alright.

'Thank you. I've never had a nicer meal.' It was true. Sitting there, in that village which I couldn't find on a map. With people who I'd never met in my life before, eating food the likes of which I didn't even know, all those unknowns together and I felt at home. Really at home. I was with people like me, family.

Finally, time to go home. I'm thinking of the old clinic as home? Must think about that. I roll round the compound, shake hands, say bye-bye to everyone, male and female, young and old. A couple of the girls who are doing the dishes, giggling, splashing everything in sight, offer me their elbows to shake. I promise everyone that I will return, that I have been very well fed, that I will take care crossing the road. Fatima will see me safely delivered back to Sirra. The compound gate screeches closed behind us. Hank is waiting in the shade of a huge tree fifty metres from the gate.

'Told you he loves you; he has been there all day' Fatou said.

'Hello, lovely. Just checking you're OK' I am furious. He's spying on me. He doesn't trust me. I'm safer here than I feel back in Cheshire.

'I thought I could trust you to trust me' I yell at him. 'Do you spy on me all the time I'm not in bed with you? You're a sick, jealous bastard. That's why you wanted to travel with me? Don't lie. I thought love meant freedom, honesty? Do I spy on you when you're in a different class at college? Do I? No, I trust you. It doesn't even cross my mind to imagine that you're a scheming, devious, duplicitous, ignorant, treacherous, lying scumbag. I loved you. I loved you. Did you win a bet that you wouldn't bed me? Did you? How much did you win? Five pounds, was that it? I've had a lovely day; a lovely, happy day and you ruin it. I'll never speak to you again. I'll sleep on the floor if I have to. Get your stuff out of my room. Now, do it now. Sod off.' I'm not crying. I don't cry over stupid, ignorant scum. I hate him.

Fatou was staring at me.

'You hate a man who loves you so much he sits in the heat of the sun all day to make sure you're safe? How can that be? I wish I had such a man. Do not throw him away,

Jodie. Do not do this. Eat your words and apologise.' Nobody understood. Nobody. I rushed at racing speed across the hot sand, straight across the road, narrowly avoiding oblivion under the wheels of a sand lorry, on across the open ground surrounding the new clinic building and into my room in the old clinic. When the tears stopped I opened the tin shutter that covered the window space and threw everything I could find of his out. The goats could have them, the dogs could run away with them. The children could dress up, the thieves could steal them, and Fatou could have him and keep him if she thought he was so bloody wonderful. Sirra brought the things back into the room and placed them carefully on the bed. My bed. She sat down and waited. I can play that game. We faced each other. Time passed.

'Well?'

'Well what?'

'Why are you pretending to be four years old?'

'I'm not.'

'Jodie, I know you're not. What's upset you?'

'I'm not upset.'

'Ah, this is your normal manner? Odd that I've not noticed it before.' She moved off the bed and knelt on the floor beside me. She put her arms round me. I struggled for a moment, then the tears came again. She waited.

'Hank's betrayed me. I thought he trusted me. He's just the same as Max. Are all men the same? I hate him. I hate him. I'll never trust a man again. A man betrayed my mum, my birth mum. She loved me. It's me. I'm no good. If I was any good they'd respect me. I'm crippled and my heart's broken.' Sirra just hugged me, and waited. She stroked my hair. I hated her doing that. Max had done that, Hank had too. A reminder of betrayal.

'Sirra, don't do that, please. Bad memories.'

'Sorry. Sorry. Didn't you know that Hank was watching out for you?'

'He didn't need to. I can look after myself. I've had to, ever since I was seven. I don't need him. I don't need anyone.'

'That's a lonely world you'll live in, Jodie. Think about it.'

'Nothing to think about. He's a rat. All men are rats.'

'He's a man, Jodie. A disabled man who loves you. A man in a wheelchair, just like you. A man who travelled thousands of miles to be with you. A man surrounded by strangers, it's his first visit here, remember. He sees hundreds of young, beautiful, athletic men and among them he sees you, vulnerable like he's vulnerable. So he watches over you. Even though he can't protect you, even though there's no need to protect you, he wants to. He sits in the shade of a Baobab tree watching out for you. If you love him why not offer him a drink of water? Why not a smile? Why not call him to share your meal? You offered him words: cruel words. I hear the words you spoke; would he ever, ever, speak like that to you? Could you not have smiled and thanked him, and explained that you were safe? I have a man, a man of your people, who has protected me for years. He's human, irritating, stubborn, well-intentioned, with sometimes annoying results. I expect he doesn't find me delightful all the time, but we talk. We talk in bed and we make love in bed and, maybe, he'll die as he sleeps in my bed. There were days when I wish that I might die there, in his arms. But I never regretted a day in his company. He cares for me even when I don't need it. But I accept his gift. I can't tell you what to do, I'm not you. But you are you, and you can change this story, if you want to. Your story, Jodie. Let us go and cook Ataya.' She got to her feet, grimacing slightly, a hand in the small of her back. She looked at me, and walked out onto the veranda.

It was very difficult to follow her. It was impossible not to. I compromised; I wheeled out very slowly. Sirra had the little charcoal stove going. On a tin tray were a small enamel tea-pot, two glasses, a packet of gunpowder tea, a jar of white sugar, and a sprig of mint. The complete kit.

'Stay and watch. Then next time you will cook.' I waited and watched, but my thoughts were elsewhere. Somewhere a couple of hundred metres and a thousand light years away. Could I admit that Hank's actions were based on love, not jealousy? How could I unsay hasty words? Did I want to, even? Wasn't there a poem about it? "The moving finger writes and then moves on. Not all your piety or wit can cancel out a word of it?" Something like that, anyway. I closed my eyes, and wished, maybe prayed.

'Jodie; do you see more clearly when your eyes are closed? Sometimes it happens that way. Listen to your heart, brains can be confused, sometimes. He's here, Jodie. Bring another glass from your room for him. Please.'

We sat in a row on the veranda; Sirra, Hank, me. We drank tea. Sirra offered Hank the first glass but he passed it to me and Sirra smiled. We carefully chatted about small things and I knew we could talk together, in bed, about serious things.

Shows how little I know. After an hour Hank drained the last of the Ataya, and announced

'Thanks, Sirra. Ed's invited me to stay at your house tonight. Hope you don't mind? I think I'll turn in early. The sun got to me, I think. Should have had more sense.' He smiles at us, then wheels off to the compound across the road. Bastard. What's wrong with my bed, our bed? I thought he must have forgiven me, sharing Ataya, chatting away about how the clinic would work, how a good team would be essential, all that sort of crap. The sun got to him? He hadn't needed to be in the sun. Why couldn't he just wheel into Amadou's compound and shout "Hi, Jodie. I've come to spy on you?" Why did he have to sleep across the road? There's a spare bed in the room next to mine. Did he think I'd go mad and kill him? I'll kill him.

Sirra looks a bit shocked. Maybe she can read my thoughts? Maybe she's surprised finding out what a rat he is? Binta and Alison arrive, hot from the kitchen.

'I thought I saw Hank? Dinner's ready, he won't want to miss this!' There's a silence. 'Hank's eating out tonight. He's sleeping out tonight. He's left.' There's a longer silence. Binta whispers something to Sirra then slips away. Alison's standing there, mouth open, gawping first at me then at Sirra.

'We've cooked a huge meal' she says.

'Take it across the road to the huge bastard' I say. Sirra stands up.

'Alison, you should know that Jodie and Hank are experiencing a difference of opinion. There is right on both sides and there is wrong on both sides. Sometimes it is necessary to experience such things so that wisdom may flourish.' She too walked away, across the compound, closing the gate behind her. Alison pulled a chair close to me and put her arm round my shoulders. I shrugged it off. Then I saw it was the one without the hand and felt worse than before. How do you explain that an action may not have been triggered for an obvious reason? Alison was crying. Bugger.

'Alison, it's me, not you. Please don't cry. I'm a bit touchy just now.' That's a brilliant choice of words. Kill me now. 'I've behaved really badly to Hank. I bawled him out for being jealous, for not trusting me, for spying on me. And I was wrong; he was just being caring. Caring as sensitively as a bulldozer, but caring. I said some dreadful things to him. He came back to the compound, sat with us, then said he was going to sleep at Sirra's house. He walked off, just like that. Didn't look back. I've lost him.'

'Go after him.

'I can't. How can I?

'Jodie, if you're half as upset as you say, you'll go. He's a brilliant guy. If I wasn't taken, I'd have him. Fatou from across the road came and talked to us. She's baffled by what you shouted at him. She'd take him off your hands, no worries. I'm not joking: go!' There were fourteen thousand reasons why I couldn't go. I could only think of two reasons for going after him. I loved him and I wanted him back. That's two. I pointed my chair for the gate and went. The gate was a struggle. The bloody chair kept bogging down in the sand. The gate into Sirra's compound was wide open. Lights blazed out. The veranda was wide, steps and a ramp led up. Four chairs, dining chairs, stood round a table. A spotless white table cloth, white china, shiny cutlery, crystal water glasses. Candles flickered behind cut glass shades. Name cards. Sirra. Ed. Hank. Jodie.

'Evening, Miss Jodie. I'll tell them you've arrived. Please join us for the meal?'

'Evening, Mr Edwards. Thank you, I will.'

When Hank and I got to bed, much, much later, we decided to have an experimental session. We wouldn't speak till daylight. You can't believe how well it worked.

40

It wasn't our last difference of opinion. I don't know how I expected a relationship to work. To be fair, I hadn't had much opportunity to observe any sort of relationship. Mum and I had got on well, I think. Sue and Bill seemed to rub along pretty well. They didn't seem to row at all. How did they manage that? They just seemed easy with one another. Giggles could be heard from their bedroom quite frequently. Couldn't be sex, they were far too old. Anyway, sex isn't funny. How can it be? Maybe they just lie there, swapping jokes. That could be good. I don't know any jokes. Perhaps I could ask Hank to tell me a joke and then I could tell it back to him. That might work. Still, even if all we ever do is to lie close to one another, and fumble around a bit and tell jokes, that would be good. And being with Hank is good, mostly. He can be bloody infuriating sometimes, and sometimes it's impossible to say exactly what he's done to be infuriating, and that's even more annoying.

Anyway, we're still in Africa. We've got identity cards and driving licences and we're tax exempt. Wheelchairs! I forget, what with all this relationship nonsense, to write about the chairs. Hank's dad had packed a container full of begged, scrounged and possibly stolen wheelchairs, crutches, a couple of hospital beds, two generators, a stack of stuff that might come in handy – plumbing and electrical stuff – and sealed the container so well it took a day to open it.

Lots of the chairs were rejects, bits missing, lacking wheels, useless tyres, that sort of thing. I got quite upset and stormed around swearing and shouting and being a general pain in the arse. I'm good at that. Meanwhile, Hank and the girls were sussing out what needed doing. Binta was amazing; she took charge of the restoration project. Alison cooked, supplied gallons of builder's tea, and fed us. She'd really got the hang of running a transport café.

Katie was a mechanical genius. She'd put all the wheelchairs which were basket cases on one side and the lined up the rest The line stretched twice round the store room. She'd select one of these and talk to it. Honestly. Mad as a very mad thing. She'd greet it, in Mandinka, and then tell it how she was going to repair it. She said it was to help her think of solutions. I honestly think she thought she was talking to the chairs. Then she'd ask the chair to point to where there might be one of the wrecked chairs which had the necessary parts available. She'd potter about the room, asking 'Is it this one? No? This one? Right.' And collect her spanners and things and dismantle the donor chair, thank it, and fit the salvaged parts to the poorly patient. Look! She's got me writing daft things now. But it worked. The patient would leave the clinic as good as new. As soon as it was fit for service Katie and Fatou, the Fatou from across the road, would take it to the home of somebody who needed it, show them how to use it safely and how to look after it. I wasn't allowed to go with them because I might set a bad example. Me, set a bad example? Really. What gave them that idea, I wonder. It might be because Hank and me we set up a chair racing stable. So because I thought it might be a good idea to get fun from being on wheels. Folk like us don't want to be pitied, that's no fun. But if we're seen enjoying our wheels, doing something other people can't do, well, that's good. By the time we had twenty chairs in service we had a racing club. Even the four old grannies joined in. They were wicked; they were willing to shed blood. They did, to be honest, get a bit puffed and I worried about them popping their clogs, so we raced them as a relay team and they were unbeatable. I was the only one who could beat them but I suspect they allowed me to win out of politeness. Hank never beat them. 'Where's their respect for me?' he wanted to know.

Another container arrived, similarly stocked to the first one. We moved this one to Lamin Village where it provided chairs and things to a few of the other surrounding villages. Katie found a local guy who was a talented welder. He converted the first container to a coolly insulated office block, with a small bedroom for a caretaker. We called him a caretaker but the locals called him a guard. Whatever, nothing went missing. We found out that he'd moved his girlfriend in to comfort him, he said. She joined us as an assistant to Alison. It all seemed to work rather well. We'd been wondering what to do with the second container. Hank's dad had been very generous but these things cost money. The guard's girl, her name was Fatou, it seems that the eldest girl in a Mandinka family is usually named Fatou, came from a family who were very talented weavers and tie-dyers. A couple were wood carvers, specialising in making very lifelike models of dancers. So, and this was another of Katie's ideas, why not stuff the container with their work and send it back to Hank's dad? His dad could market it and keep a quarter of the profit. The carvers and weavers and dyers could have the rest and we would charge ten per cent for expenses. It worked.

Fatou wanted to trade under the name 'Crafty Africa' but we persuaded her to think of something else. She wasn't happy. 'But we are African, we are proud to be African. And we are crafty; we work hard at our crafts, we are proud of our skills; we are crafty. We are Crafty Africa. What's wrong with that?' We hadn't the heart to tell her, and maybe she was right. Hank's dad reported that the stuff sold well and people laughed when they saw the name. So, what do I know?

It seemed that the new President had heard of our work and sent some sort of official to inspect us. He went through our accounts and seemed puzzled. 'Why do you do this work? Where does the profit go? You are trading drugs?' It took ages to convince him that we did the work because we liked to, wanted to, and got kick out of seeing how a proper wheelchair could change people's lives. They changed from begging to working, to becoming athletes, to gaining respect. He looked at us, at Hank and me, and frowned.

'But you are not cripples. Why do you pretend? I think you can walk and run and dance. It is evil to pretend to be cripples. It is very deceitful.' I was getting angry. Hank stopped my intended assault on the guy.

'Jodie, could you find Alison, please? Perhaps if she spoke to this gentleman he would gain understanding?' Really? Perhaps if I ran over his feet and did wheelies across his stomach he'd gain understanding. I wheeled off to the kitchen and explained Hank's idea to the girls. Ali seemed doubtful. 'If you and Hank can't change his mind how can I?'

'Remember that obnoxious woman in the coffee shop? Why not serve him a nice cool drink, Malta, perhaps. And a plate of home-made cake? See if he thinks you're a fake too?'

Binta and Alison loaded a tray with glasses and plates. Ali carried it into the work room and, balancing the tray on one arm handed out drinks and plates to all of us. The doubting man, took a glass, set it down on a ledge, and helped himself to a plate and a couple of cakes. Ali took hold of the tray with her good hand, smiled at him, and offered the tray to me. I introduced her, and saw his eyes register that the hand holding the tray was the only one she possessed. Try faking that, clever clogs. I didn't say the words but he looked at me and frowned. His eyes moved to Binta. I could see the cogs working. 'That one looks normal. Is she faking being normal?' He looked at his glass, now filled with Malta poured by Ali. She grinned at him. We held our breath. The he smiled. 'Hank, Alison, Binta, Jodie, I apologise. I heard so many good things about your work that I suspected you were running some complicated scam, some way of cheating people, some form of deceitfulness. Such people do exist, yes; even white people who pretend to help but really pretend charity to either enrich their pockets or their egos. I apologise. Please, if you can, forgive me?' A pause, then Ali reached out her arm and without a moments pause, he held it in both his hands and smiled at her. 'Sister, I greet you. Thank you for showing me my mistake. Alison placed her hand over his.

'Don't worry about it, chuck. Anyone can be wrong, but it takes a proper chap to admit it.' I don't think he'd ever been called 'chuck' before, but he didn't die of shock. He shook all our hands, total of seven, again and helped himself to another cake. 'These are excellent. Miss Binta, did you cook these?'

'No, sir. Miss Alison was teaching me to bake but these were made by her.' He licked his lips and Ali poured him another drink.

'Miss Alison, I have a proposal for you and your team.' Her team? Hank put his finger to his lips. Why am I always being told to shut up? The minx was smiling at him.

'I wonder if you have time to act as a cookery consultant to my ministry. I would pay you a wage, and all your expenses, and I will make sure that your charity is never bothered for payment of registration fees. Hank, sir, does this sound good to you? Can you spare Miss Alison for just one month?' He's bloody asking Hank! Perhaps if I gibber a bit and drool he'll notice me? Hank's looking at me, nodding. Bloody donkey. They're all looking at me. Oh, look, I'm a nodding donkey too. Nod nod nod. 'Thank you. Miss Alison, if I send a car for you, Monday, perhaps? At what time?'

'Thank you, sir. As early as possible, perhaps? Say. Five in the morning? I can examine your kitchen, order food, and meet the staff? Then we can prepare your breakfast?' Creeping little cow. I'll kill her first, as soon as his majesty's taken himself off. He's looking at me.

'Miss Jodie, sister, I congratulate you. You are doing a wonderful thing for us, for our country. I have learned a valuable lesson today, that wonderful people, like you and your talented team, are creating a new life for people. You give them hope, you inspire them, especially you and Mr Hank and Miss Alison. I hope to visit you many more times, and, as a token of my respect for you and your work, may I now make a donation of ten thousand dalasi, to be used by your team to further your work here? Miss Jodie, I have heard of your work in the University, helping to educate our wonderful generation of young women. May I invite you to act as consultant advisor to the department of further education? There is a small salary attached to the position, which I am sure you will use wisely. And Mr Hank, may I offer you a similar situation in the department of Physical Education? I apologise, I must rush off and report to His Excellency. He is most anxious to know my thoughts concerning your excellent endeavours.'

He rushed so rapidly he was only able to accept another bottle of Malta and all the remaining cakes from the hand of his new cookery advisor. Must keep an eye on that relationship. She could poison the whole government if they piss her off. Never argue with your cook. And get Hank. Trust him to get the PE job. He's looking at me. They're all looking at me. 'What? Have I got snot on my chin?'

'Three cheers for Jodie! Hip, hip, hooray!'

'Idiots. Why?'

'You handled that brilliantly! Well done you! Really got it right.' They'd gone mad.

'Why, what did I do? I hardly said a word!'

'Yes, brilliant.' I'll kill the lot of them. Slowly. Oh, here's Ali with more cakes. Maybe I'll delay sentencing.

41

Mum and dad finally made it to The Old Clinic. The nameplate looked good. One of the Crafty Africans made it for us. It looked like a piece of modern sculpture, all twisting and writhing bits of driftwood and chromium strips off wrecked cars and lengths of contorted brass piping. But, if you were in exactly the right spot it spelled out the name. Clear as daylight: The Old Clinic. Move a bit to one side or the other and nothing. Like getting something into focus. I loved it. The aged parents were blown away. I introduced them to the Crafty people. Mistake, big time. They're never getting all the stuff they purchased home, let alone the stuff they were given. We sorted it out when we shipped the third container home. They stayed for a month.

'You're not coming home, are you, Jodie?'

'Not yet, mum. There's too much going on. Not just with the charity and the teaching and the people. Inside my head. I've stopped thinking of me as a useless fucking cripple.'

'Jodie!'

'Sorry mum, it's true. You know that Stone Age scraper thing I had? Well, I've still got it. And now I'm here, and I've met young Fatou Manneh,'

'That's the girl who makes toys?'

'Yes, that's her. Now I've met her and seen her making tools, I know I'm part of it. I don't properly know what "it" is yet, but I'm belonging to something, like a tribe or a race of people. It's here, being in this village. I'm here, and it's here, in my blood. You know that DNA test you can do, to prove your ancestry? Well, I don't need to take a test, and all the other people I meet here, they know it too. I'm part of a tradition that goes back thousands of years, survived Ice Ages and Continental Drift and famines and desertification and lots of other things I don't even know about, and it's like the things I've survived, as a child, loss of mum, rape, accidents, it all sort of fits together, like a jigsaw. I don't even like jigsaws, but this one fits because I'm part of it. And because I'm part of it, I'm important. I owe it something. Maybe I can have children who'll pass "it" on, maybe I can't. But whatever, I can contribute something, show people that folk like me and Hank and Ali, are important and equal. Maybe we're only tiny parts of it, like grains of sand in a desert. But if we didn't exist it wouldn't be the same desert. And because it exists we're important grains of sand.'

I was silent for a while. I couldn't believe I'd said all that. I hated some of it, it sounded so big-headed and stupid, but mum was staring at me, smiling. We hugged, awkwardly. Hugging a wheelchair can be bloody awkward. But, she was smiling.

'Jodie, love, I'm so proud of you. We both are. We love you. You are a very important grain of sand. The image suits you. Grains of sand can be terribly irritating, but you're our grain of sand, and we love you.'

You should be bloody careful going through sliding doors. You never know where they'll lead you.

42 Possible final Chapter, just for the moment.

Well, that's my tale told, at least for the moment. I'm still, in many people's eyes, that same list of letters and numbers we started off with. I'm actually a little lighter and a lot fitter than I was then. I'm getting used to being called names and pushed out of the way by people who consider themselves to be more important human beings than I am. Perhaps I should have taken that title I was offered. I also get abuse for being a member of a political party, mostly from members of the same party. The abuse is based on that same collection of letters and numerals.

I didn't win a Paralympic Gold Medal and I never did get a degree. Well, I did eventually get an honorary one but that doesn't count. I didn't get either because I was too busy seducing Hank, and I've now got him and a gorgeous baby girl called Fatou Jodie Sonko because that's how we Mandinka women name our first girl child.

I've just read through this manuscript again, last time before it goes out to meet its readers. Hope you enjoy it. It is going to join a series of books about my village, my adopted village, Malinding. I think it's the eighth book in the series. I've read most of them now. I started with the first one, Empty Bananas, which is mainly about Ed, Sirra's husband. I didn't like him from the book but he's really OK when you get to know him. Oddly, and how strange is this, I'd met him when I was a little girl. You remember the day when I ran away from a foster home and went to sit by the canal? Ed was the man on that little boat, the guy who gave me a can of Coke. Strange, the way the world works.

Well, that's fifty-five and a half thousand words, and I'll leave it there for now. Thanks for reading my story. One more thing to tell you: all the money from the sale of these books goes into a charity account – Gambian Occasional Emergency Support. They helped our little charity too, when we ran out of money.

Printed in Great Britain
by Amazon